CLAWS FOR ALARM

A Gray Whale Inn
MYSTERY

KAREN MACINERNEY

Cover Design and Interior Format

© THE KILLION GROUP, INC.

OTHER BOOKS IN THE GRAY WHALE INN MYSTERIES

CHAPTER ONE

"**I**'M GOING TO KILL HER," Charlene fumed, stabbing her apple kuchen with a fork. The afternoon light had turned my yellow kitchen walls gold, and a cool breeze wafted through the open window.

"Whoa there," I said. "Francine's just trying to make the island look better." The garden-obsessed Floridian and her husband had recently bought a house on Cranberry Island, and Francine Hodges had immediately directed her prodigious energy to turning the island into something that belonged in *House and Garden* magazine. "Besides," I reminded her, "they're summer people. She'll be gone soon enough."

"Soon enough? We've got months to go," she said. "She doesn't go back to Florida until October. By that time, she'll have the lupine field turned into the front lawn of Versailles and Claudette's goats turning on a spit."

"There might be a few people who wouldn't mind that," I pointed out. "Those goats have rampaged many a garden on Cranberry Island. Ingrid Sorenson's been replacing her geraniums biweekly for years. Besides," I added jokingly—I was rather fond of Muffin and Pudge, after all—"Cabrito's pretty good, especially on tacos. It's a Texas specialty."

"I hear they have breakfast tacos in Texas, too." Charlene wrinkled her nose. "Sounds kind of gross."

"Oh, they're not," I said. I didn't miss many things about Texas—I'd moved to Maine from Austin and bought the Gray Whale Inn a few years back and had never looked back—but I did miss Mexican food, particularly breakfast tacos. And Blue Bell ice cream. "I'll make you some soon," I promised. "The salsa might be a little hot for your northern palate, but there's nothing wrong with eggs, potatoes, and melted cheese on a fresh tortilla."

"Sounds passable," she admitted. "But back to Francine. How are we going to keep her from trying to turn the island into a picture postcard?" She leaned forward. "She was after me to take all the notices off the front window of the store the other day. Said it looked 'messy.'"

"What did you tell her?" I asked. Charlene was the postmistress and owner of the island's store, which also functioned as the island's living room. The front part was filled with squashy couches where locals drank coffee and exchanged news, and the windows were always plastered with notices of local goings-on.

"I said I'd think about it, which I did for about two seconds. And did you know she wants the lobster co-op to stop loading traps on the dock? Says the bait smell is a problem for visitors getting off the mail boat."

"Seriously?"

"Seriously. She plans to bring it up at the next town meeting."

"I'll bring popcorn," I said. "What else is going on? How are things with you and Alex?"

Charlene and Alex, a talented photographer and naturalist, had started dating earlier in the summer, when a schooner nature tour had made the inn home base.

She sighed. "Well, Alex is working in Alaska this summer, so I won't see him till the fall, but things are going great. We talk every night."

"I'm glad," I said. "It's about time you met someone wonderful."

"Yeah. It's just too bad he's on the other side of the world. I was thinking I might fly down to see him for a few days this winter."

I took a bite of my own kuchen and nodded my approval. "Sounds like a good plan to me."

"November might be a good time. It depends on what his schedule is. And we'll see about Christmas…"

"Holidays can be weird when you haven't been dating long, can't they?"

"They can," she agreed. "Especially when it's long-distance." She toyed with a bit of apple on her plate. "And speaking of romance, how are things going with Gwen and Adam?" My niece and her lobsterman boyfriend had gotten engaged, and there was talk of a wedding in the fall, but the date was still kind of uncertain.

"She's supposedly planning the wedding, but she's been so busy doing workshops, trekking back and forth to the art studio on the mainland, and helping me out here that I don't think she's made much progress."

"Maybe she should push it out to the spring and figure it out this winter," Charlene suggested.

"I think they're anxious to get the show on the road," I said. "They'd like to move in together, and I get the feeling they may be thinking of starting a family."

"Oh my gosh," Charlene said, her eyes getting wide. "That would be so amazing! You'd be Aunt Nat to a munchkin! Do you think she'd let me be Aunt Char?"

I laughed. "I think she'll have a whole island full of aunts and uncles if she decides to have children. But in the meantime, we should probably see if we can help her get down the aisle."

"I love weddings," Charlene sighed. "I wonder what kind of dress she's getting? I was looking at a few strapless Vera Wangs the other day..."

"You were looking at wedding gowns?"

My friend blushed and stabbed at her kuchen again. "I've always wanted a wedding," she confessed.

"I know," I said, reaching out to touch her arm. "But take your time, please. You haven't known Alex that long."

She waved me away. "It's kind of hard to marry someone when you never see him in person, so you don't need to worry. Speaking of halfway around the world, I hear you're cooking Indian style this week."

"Not exactly," I said. "They originally wanted all vegetarian food, but I talked them into a good bit of lobster and fish." I shrugged. "After all, this is Maine."

"Not a lot of coffee cakes?"

"I got them to compromise. I tried a giant tofu scramble this morning at Willow's request. So far, there hasn't exactly been a run on the tofu, but the coffee cake is going down awfully fast." I grimaced. "I probably should work on eating healthier myself; I run around all the time, but all this good food is catching up with me." I pulled up my T-shirt and showed her the top button of my jeans, which no longer met the buttonhole, and which I'd resorted to fastening with an elastic band.

"Sexy," Charlene said.

"Yeah, well, I haven't had a lot of time to go shopping."

"I'm just teasing," Charlene said. "But I'll bet a week of tofu scramble would do the trick."

"No, thank you," I said. "Moderation, not masochism, is my motto."

At that moment, there was a knock at the kitchen door; soon after, Willow, the yoga retreat leader, shimmered into the room.

When she'd called to set up the retreat, I'd imagined a wispy, tall, Gwyneth Paltrowesque woman—the kind who disappears when she turns sideways. Willow, despite her high, reedy voice, looked more like an MMA fighter than a supermodel. She didn't just have abs of steel; she had everything of steel, all packed into a solid frame that was just over five feet tall, along with a halo of black corkscrew curls she pulled back from her face with a purple bandanna. Her coffee-colored skin was flawless: not a scar or blemish to be seen. Maybe there *was* something to the whole vegan lifestyle after all.

"How's it going out there?" I asked.

"Oh, it's been a brilliant day," she said in that incongruously breathy voice. She moved into something like tree pose—I'd tried it once in a yoga class in Austin—and picked an invisible piece of lint off her pale green spandex crop top. The movement made her six-pack ripple. "It's just so peaceful out; we're about to go meditate on the lawn."

"Sounds lovely," I said. "Willow, this is my friend Charlene. Charlene, this is Willow; she's running the yoga retreat."

"Nice to meet you," Charlene said as she took Willow's firm extended hand. "And I hope you don't mind my saying so, but I had no idea yoga could make you so fit; you look amazing!"

"Oh, yoga is just wonderful on so many levels," Willow said. "You're welcome to come join us for one of the sessions!"

"Really?" Charlene looked both excited and dubious.

"Why don't you come over for the sunset yoga session?" Willow suggested.

"I think I might do that. I don't have a yoga mat or anything."

"You can borrow one of mine," she offered.

"Green tea and kale smoothies at three?" I asked. She nodded. "That would be perfect," she said.

"I'll have it lined up in the dining room," I told her.

"If you'd like to join us for a session, you're always welcome," she offered. "Both of you, in fact."

"Think I could manage it without keeling over?" Charlene asked.

"Of course," she said. "And you can always modify the posture. We've got a relaxing one an hour after dinner tonight; it's not too strenuous, if you want to just try it out."

"Thanks," I said. "I might take you up on it."

"If it means I could have abs like yours, I'll try it," Charlene said.

Willow laughed. "I've got to go help Sequoia get things set up." She beamed at Charlene, flashing her ivory white teeth. "Hope to see you after dinner!"

"Wow," Charlene said once she'd left the kitchen. "She's gorgeous."

"I know."

"But what's with the tree names?" Charlene asked. "Do you pick your magical forest name when you get your yoga instructor certification?"

"I'd probably be Stumpy," I joked.

"And with my dating history, I'd be Hemlock," she said with a wry grin. Her previous beaux had had a rather high mortality rate. The grin faded. "I haven't told Alex about what happened."

"Unless there's something you haven't told me about and you're a closet serial killer," I said, "I don't see how it matters."

"You don't think I'm... jinxed?"

I shook my head vehemently. "I think you've had some bad luck. And I think it's about to change. As long as you take things slowly, that is."

She sighed. "Hard not to. Man, these long-distance relationships are tough. If he had an actual home, I'd be tempted to move."

"Don't even think about it," I warned her half-jokingly. I couldn't imagine living on Cranberry Island without Charlene. "There's plenty of room for Alex here... if things work out."

"Why are you so down on Alex today?"

"I'm not," I said. "I'm just... I care about you. I want you to make sure he's the right one."

"All right, Mom," she said, sliding off her chair. "Need help with the smoothies?"

"Sure," I said. "I wouldn't suggest drinking them, though."

"If drinking them would make me look like Willow, I could be convinced," she said. And then I put a bag of kale, two cucumbers, and a canister of soy protein next to the blender. "Or maybe not," she added, looking somewhat horrified.

"There are a few leftover chocolate chip cookies in the jar if you're interested," I suggested.

"Thanks." She walked over and snagged two. "After all, I'll work these off at yoga tonight, right?"

🌿 🌿

At three on the dot, I had a dozen glasses of green sludge on a tray, ready to go, along with an assortment of seaweed snacks for the yoga retreat participants. Although Willow and Sequoia put on wholesome-looking smiles when I stepped out of the kitchen, most of the rest of my guests seemed to share Charlene's misgivings at what was on the tray. Except for James, who was a tall, ultrafit Cross-Fit type who seemed to survive on bacon and kale. I had to admit it was working for him; he looked like he belonged in *GQ*, if *GQ* did photo shoots of men in yoga pants.

"What's in it?" he asked, gazing at me with serious hazel eyes.

"Soy protein, kale, and cucumbers," I said.

"Not whey protein?"

"Sorry," I said.

"Soy has a lot of benefits," Willow said brightly.

"And lectins," James added. I wasn't sure what lectins were, but evidently, they were some kind of dietary evil on a par with mercury. Ah, James. He was good to look at but didn't appear to be fabulous company—at least not for me.

"Next time we'll make yours with whey protein," Willow assured him.

"I'd love to hear about lectins," Kellie, one of a trio of young mothers from Dallas, piped up. She was bright and perky, with purple yoga pants and a tight-fitting matching top. Although she sported a rather large diamond ring and a matching wedding band on her left hand, she had been flirting with James since she arrived. Unfortunately for her, I wasn't sure he'd noticed.

"Lectins," he began, "are a protein that seeds use to protect themselves. When we eat them, our bodies produce antibodies to them. That's why it's advisable to eat sprouted grains, which don't have lectins."

"Fascinating," she said, blinking her long lashes at him. I think she was talking more about the view than the lecture. "Are there lectins in vodka?"

"No," he said. "But if you're going to indulge in spirits, vodka is one of the best choices—in moderation, of course. Definitely not beer, though."

"Good. Because I'd kill for some vodka right now," said Kellie, taking a sip of kale-cucumber sludge. "Maybe it would cover up the soy protein, or whatever it is in this."

"Vodka would be so awesome," agreed her sidekick, Barbara Sue. She wore an almost identical outfit, only in teal, and not quite to the same advantage. Both women were coiffed perfectly, with honey-blond locks that looked as if they'd been ironed. The third of the trio looked a little out of place with her friends; she had on an oversize T-shirt and a pair of compression shorts with a streak of yellow paint on the left thigh, and her slightly curly brown hair was pulled back in a ponytail. She passed on the green sludge, instead taking a sip from a water bottle.

I glanced around at the rest of the room. The yoga cabal, as I thought of them privately—Willow and her waiflike assistants, Sequoia and Rainy—who looked like she still belonged in high school—were sprinkled through the room, all wearing organically sourced formfitting yoga attire. As I watched, Rainy winked at Ravi, her boyfriend, who was sharing a room with her and was, from what I could see, kind of in-and-out at the retreat. He had long, silky black locks that framed his high-cheekboned face and large, liquid eyes. I had the feeling Rainy was the jealous type; she tended to fret when he wasn't around, and I noticed her watching when he talked with the other female participants—particularly Kellie.

"Is there any vegetable juice?" asked Sebastian in a doleful voice.

I glanced at Willow, who was frowning. She had originally been picky about the food and drink offerings, but I was in the business of hospitality. "I've got cranberry juice, orange juice, and apple juice," I offered. "There are also a variety of teas and a kettle, if you're interested."

"I could go for a Pimm's Cup," Gage said, flopping back in his chair as if he'd just finished a stage of the Tour de France. Unlike Sebastian, who wore sweatpants and a Portland T-shirt, Gage had stylish track pants and a muscle shirt that showed off his trim physique. Unlike James, however, he clearly hadn't sworn off the mixed drinks. "That Pimm's Cup was divine... with a little bit of cucumber and strawberry, just like we had in the Monteleone in New Orleans... remember, Bastian?"

"I remember I had to practically carry you up to our room," Sebastian sniffed.

"Nonsense." Gage waved him away. Gage and Sebastian were a testament to the opposites-attract school of relationship theory. Where Gage seemed to be the human equivalent of Tigger, Sebastian appeared to be channeling Eeyore. "I was the life of the party!" Gage protested. "We only went home because you were tired."

Sebastian turned to me. "Do you have any chamomile tea?"

"I'll get you a cup," I said, and turned to Gage. "Anything for you?"

"You don't have any Pimm's No. 1 hiding back there in the kitchen, do you?"

"I'm afraid not," I said. "I might be able to find some wine for dinner, though."

He snuck an exaggerated glance at Willow and Sequoia. "Meet me out back when the cock crows twice," he said in a stage whisper.

"Roosters don't crow at night," Sebastian pointed out.

I laughed. "I don't think they'll throw you out of

the retreat if you have a glass of wine with dinner."

"I don't know about that," Gage said, raising his eyebrows. "Have you talked with Sequoia?"

I hadn't—not much anyway. Sequoia was the behind-the-scenes organizer. Most of my contact had been with Willow. "I'll talk with them about flexibility. Think positive. I got them to okay coffee cake, after all."

"I wish you luck," Gage said earnestly, fixing me with his bright blue eyes. As I finished serving the rest of the drinks, the phone rang. I hurried to the kitchen to pick up.

"Natalie! Thank God you're there." It was my best friend, Charlene.

"What's wrong?"

"Claudette and Francine just got into a food fight at the store!"

"What?"

"Oh my gosh. Claudette just hit her over the head with a gallon of soy milk. Hurry!"

CHAPTER TWO

WE WERE IN MY VAN in forty-five seconds flat.

"Soy milk?" John asked as I gunned the engine and headed up the driveway. As the island deputy, he was frequently called upon to deal with altercations, but this was the first time I could remember anything involving dairy products. Or nondairy products, actually.

"I guess it was handy," I said.

"What are they fighting about?"

"If I had to guess, I suspect Francine took issue with the boat graveyard in front of the Whites' house."

"I can imagine she wouldn't be a fan," John said.

"Either that," I hypothesized, "or she decided to take the issue of Muffin and Pudge into her own hands."

"She wouldn't hurt Claudette's goats, would she?"

"Have you ever seen two goats chained to a tire gracing the cover of *Coastal Living Magazine*?"

"I don't read *Coastal Living Magazine*."

I gave him a look.

"But no, I imagine not," he said hastily.

I could see the soy milk dripping down the inside of the window when we pulled up outside of the Cranberry Island General Store.

"Hey, at least the window's not broken." No sooner had the words left my mouth than a potato exploded through the top pane of the mullioned shop window. We both ducked as it bounced off the top of the van. "You first," I said.

"You're not going to be my backup?"

"You're the trained professional," I pointed out. As he reluctantly headed up the stairs to the front porch, I called after him. "Don't hurt Claudette!"

"Don't hurt Claudette? I'm not the one winging potatoes and soy milk!"

As he opened the door, I could hear Claudette yelling. "Who the hell do you think you are anyway? My family's lived on this island for over a century!"

"Well, maybe it's time for some fresh blood," Francine's higher voice responded. "Or at least someone with an understanding of basic hygiene."

"Hygiene? *Hygiene*?" The second "hygiene" was punctuated, appropriately, by a twelve-pack of toilet paper. John caught it and stepped inside, holding it out like a two-ply shield.

"Ladies," he announced in his most commanding voice, "what is going on here?"

There was a moment of silence, broken only by the sound of dripping soy milk and no further projectiles. I gauged it safe to tiptoe up the steps to where I could get a better view.

"This... this... *outsider* thinks our house doesn't fit the island's 'image,'" she said with exaggerated air quotes. Claudette, always solid, reminded me of one of the more stolid Viking goddesses, with gray braids and a frown that, frankly, I was surprised hadn't curdled what was left of the soy milk. "And she wants to *imprison* my babies."

"Muffin and Pudge?" I asked.

"Just because they eat a few flowers from time to time."

They ate more than a few flowers in my experience, but I felt this wasn't the time to mention it.

"I didn't threaten to jail your stupid goats," Francine answered in a whiny voice. "All I suggested was that you and your husband keep your derelict boats in the barn, where they belong... along with your hoofed menaces."

"Derelict boats? Hoofed menaces?" I could see Claudette's eyes leap to the nearest object, which at the moment was a row of pink toilet brushes.

"Hold on, both of you," John said, holding up his hands. "I understand you have different opinions, but let's not do any more damage to Charlene's store than we already have."

"Thanks so much for coming, John," my friend said from the back of the store, where she was crouched down behind the counter. I spotted the top of her white head first, and then the rest of her as she cautiously stood up. For a moment, I wondered if she'd had an accident at the beautician when she went for her highlight touch-up, but when she stood up, powdered sugar cascaded down her shoulders onto the counter. It looked like there'd been a blizzard. "Is it safe to come out yet?"

"I don't know," John said slowly, looking at both women. "Is it?"

Claudette took a deep breath and turned to Charlene. "I'm sorry about your store," she said. "I'll help you clean up."

"Well," Francine said, wiping the soy milk from her eyes and surveying the front of the store. "At least it means some of those notices are coming down."

"You know what, Francine?" Charlene said, coming out from around the bar in the back. "I know you mean well, or at least I think on some level you do, but you can't come in here and just change everything so it looks like something out of *Better Homes and Gardens*. We live here. We like it this way."

"I live here, too, now," Francine said. "I have a voice in how things are."

"Yes," Charlene said. "But one voice. There are a lot of other voices, too, and most of them have been here for decades."

Francine surveyed Charlene, who looked a little like a human beignet, and sniffed. "We'll see about that," she huffed, and headed to the door. "I'll be doing my shopping on the mainland from now on," she announced, and then turned to Claudette before flouncing out. "And if your ridiculous-looking goats come within ten feet of my prize hydrangeas, they'll be pushing up daisies."

"You wouldn't!" Claudette said, her face flushing. I caught her scanning the shelves for projectiles, and cleared my throat.

"Don't try me," Francine hissed, and then flounced out of the door John was holding without looking at either of us.

We watched her as she turned and marched up

the lane toward her sprawling compound.

"It's hard to look regal when you're covered in soy milk," John observed. "But points for effort."

"Wow. That was worth the price of a cup of coffee."

We all swiveled, startled. A thirtysomething woman with a mane of brown hair had materialized from behind a shelf; it was Pauline Adams.

"Pauline!" Charlene said. "I didn't realize you were still here!"

"I hid behind the dog food when things got dicey," Pauline said. "My money was on you, though, Claudette. You sure read her the riot act."

Claudette turned an even deeper shade of scarlet.

"Let's help you get this place cleaned up," I volunteered, hoping to skirt any more embarrassment. "I've got about an hour before I need to head back and think about dinner."

"No," Claudette said, brushing a bit of sugar off her broomstick skirt. "I'm responsible for this. I should be the one cleaning it all up." She let out a long breath. "I don't know what came over me. I'm embarrassed... I've never done anything like that before. I'm so sorry!"

"You were provoked," Charlene said. "And you were doing your best to stick up for me... and everyone else on this island. We'll all help," she said with a smile. "Just lay off the powdered sugar next time, okay? I'm trying to cut back."

We all burst out laughing.

"She looked like a wet hen, didn't she?" Charlene said.

"She did," I said. "Maybe she learned her lesson."

"I doubt it," Charlene said. "If anything, I'm

guessing it galvanized her."

"Let's hope not," I told her as I headed to the back to find a broom.

"Well, that was exciting," John said as we pulled out of the parking lot. We'd papered over the broken window for now, and gotten up most of the soy milk, but Charlene was going to be finding powdered sugar for weeks.

"I hope Francine doesn't press charges," I fretted as I bumped up the road toward the inn. It was late summer, and the world was beautiful and green. I took a deep breath of pine-scented air, trying to let go of my worries.

"Francine was the one winging potatoes," John said.

"Really? That wasn't Claudette?"

"She put them down in a hurry when I got to the door."

"Well, at least Claudette wasn't the only aggressor."

"Francine could claim the potatoes were used in self-defense. But let's hope it doesn't come to that."

"She should at least offer to fix the window at the store," I said. "After all, she is in to beautification. A giant mullioned window patched with part of a cardboard shipping box isn't exactly picturesque."

John reached over and patted my leg. "It'll work itself out. In the meantime, how's the retreat going?"

"Well enough, except for the fact that half the participants aren't exactly thrilled with the menu."

"Did you talk to Willow and Sequoia?"

"Not yet," I said as I crested the hill above the inn. As always, I swooned a little at the sight of the gray-shingled building with blue shutters. I still couldn't believe it was mine. Ours now, I thought, reaching over to squeeze John's hand. "Have you seen Gwen today, by the way?"

"No," he replied. "She's been on the mainland a lot the last few days." Gwen's fortunes had turned when one of the owners of the Acadia National Park gift shop had seen a watercolor series she'd done of some of the landmarks on Mount Desert Island. She'd invited her to sell prints in the shop, and Gwen had been bustling around trying to get a system in place to have prints made and her work framed ever since.

"She hasn't been painting much lately, has she?"

"I'm afraid the business side has kind of eclipsed the art," John said. He knew how that was; although he did amazing sculptures from driftwood he found on the beaches and rocky crags of Cranberry Island, like most islanders, he had multiple streams of income. Not only did he earn an income as the island's deputy, but in the summer, he did very well by crafting toy boats and other simple wooden souvenirs for Island Artists.

"For you, too, it seems," I said. He'd been spending a lot of time on what he called "production work" lately.

"It'll be September before we know it," he said. "It'll slow down, and I'll have time to get back to sculpting."

"I hope so," I said. "It's good for you."

"Everything has a season," he said. "And right

now, it's the season of toy boats and yogis."

"And flying potatoes, apparently," I said as I parked the van in the driveway.

"Who knew? On the plus side, with all this yoga and meditation, at least it should be a peaceful evening," John said.

It should have been.

But it wasn't.

John and I were clearing up the last of the smoothie glasses when the sound of raised voices wafted through the open windows of the dining room.

"Uh-oh," John said.

"Just as long as they don't start throwing potatoes."

"Soy milk is more likely with this group," he replied.

A woman's strident voice rang out. "You told me there was nothing between you. And then I find you two holed up in her room together..."

"There is nothing between us. I told you, I was teaching her how to release a trigger point."

"Uh-huh. You couldn't do that with everyone else around?"

"She needed to lie down for me to show her," the other voice said. There was a wheedling tone to it that struck a false note with me.

John and I exchanged looks. I tiptoed over to the window and peered out; it was Rainy and her boyfriend, Ravi. Her arms were crossed tightly across her body, and she looked like she was ready to spit bullets. Or soy pellets.

"You know what? I don't want you staying in the same room with me."

"What?" Ravi ran a hand through his curly hair and took a step back. "Where will I sleep?"

"Ask Kellie," she spat. "I'm sure she'd let you share." She whirled around and stormed off, leaving Ravi looking bewildered.

I stepped back from the window and raised my eyebrows at John.

"What was that all about?" he asked when we got to the kitchen.

"Lovers' quarrel between Rainy and Ravi."

"I thought yoga was supposed to make you feel all Zen, and peaceful, and loving."

"That doesn't seem to extend to significant others," I observed. "But more importantly, if she kicks Ravi out, where are we going to put him?"

"On the mainland?" John suggested.

I sighed. "It might come to that, I'm afraid. I know Gwen's spending most of her time on the mainland or with Adam, but I don't think she's quite ready for me to rent out her room." In fact, Gwen was gone so much, I was thinking I might have to hire more help.

"Have you seen her room lately? We might need a backhoe to clear it out."

I winced. "That bad?"

"She left the door open the other day when she went downstairs for a snack. It looks like a clothing donation truck had a terrible collision with an art supply store."

"So that's out," I said. "I'll just have to tell him I'm full. I hate to kick anyone out, but there's literally no room at the inn."

"It's a good problem to have in the bed-and-breakfast business," John pointed out as he finished loading the dishwasher. "Need any help getting dinner together? What are we serving tonight anyway?"

"Baked haddock with a choice of real mashed potatoes or cauliflower mashed potatoes, and a green salad," I said. "For dessert, I'll serve fresh berries for the die-hards and ice cream or sorbet for everyone else."

"I thought I heard you talking about chocolate cake," he said, looking disappointed.

"That's on this afternoon's agenda. It takes a day to chill."

"How did you get them to okay that?"

"It's got sugar but no gluten, so it was an acceptable compromise."

John glanced at his watch; dinner was less than two hours away. "We'd better get cooking."

"If you could take care of the cauliflower and the potatoes, I'll get started on the cake," I said.

"You get the chocolate, and I get the cruciferous vegetables? I see how this works."

I laughed. "Watch out, or I'll start pelting you with produce."

He grimaced. "Speaking of that, I have a feeling we haven't seen the last of Francine."

I measured salt, sugar, and water into a saucepan and turned the heat to medium. While the water heated, I pulled down a few packets of baking chocolate and opened them, counting out squares and putting them into the top of a double boiler. "If she touches those goats..."

"I've heard you threaten Muffin and Pudge a few

times yourself," John pointed out as he poured a bag of Yukon Gold potatoes into a colander.

I gave the sugar water a stir. "You know I would never hurt them. But I'm not so sure about Francine. I don't trust her as far as I can throw her."

"Where in Florida was she from?" he asked as he dumped the potatoes into a big pot on the back of the stove. His arm brushed mine, and I smiled; just touching him still sent a zing through me.

"Fort Lauderdale, I think, but I don't remember. I'll have to ask Charlene." While the chocolate melted and the water heated, I measured out the butter and prepared two cake pans.

"She really is a force of nature," John said. "I was talking to Ingrid Sorenson the other day; you know how big she is on appearances, but she wasn't a fan of Francine either."

"Good," I said. "Francine could use a little pushback. She's trying to get the town council to outlaw lobstermen stacking traps in their yards."

"She'll have better luck with that than she will getting rid of the bait smell around the pier," he said.

"How does she propose to do that?" I asked.

"A second pier for the lobstermen, on the other side of the island."

"What? That'll never pass."

"Probably not," he said. "She's got the entire lobster co-op up in arms."

"Who doesn't she have up in arms?" I stirred the now-melted chocolate and poured it into a mixer, then started beating in the butter.

"Her husband seems mild-mannered." John rinsed the cauliflower and put it into a pot, then opened the window, thankfully. I liked cauliflower, but I didn't like the way it made the kitchen smell.

"Gus, right? I haven't met him, but I've seen him around.

"I met him down at Island Artists the other day. He seemed genuinely interested in the history of the island; he asked about the inn."

"I guess they couldn't both be pistols," I said as I finished beating in the butter and slowly poured in the sugar water. "They'd kill each other."

"Maybe she'll calm down," John said. "Run out of steam or something."

"I hope so," I said as I added the eggs one by one to the batter.

"That smells amazing," John said, staring at the bowl of fudgy goodness.

"I know," I said. "Maybe I should have made a triple batch."

"There's always tomorrow," he said as I filled the pans and slid them into the oven, hoping the smell of chocolate cake baking would drown out the cruciferous tang of cauliflower.

The dining room was about as peaceful as a demilitarized zone when I brought in dinner that night; Ravi and Rainy were seated at different tables, and there seemed to have been some kind of falling-out among the Texas trio. At least Gage and Sebastian seemed to be getting along... as did Virginia and Andrew, who had become friendly rather quickly. James, too, looked normal, at least for him. I was hoping the problem with the others was carbohydrate deprivation, and that a good helping of mashed potatoes would help put everyone back into a Zen mood.

I had just finished clearing the dinner dishes and John was dishing up the sorbet when there was a knock at the door.

"I'll get it," I told John, and headed to the front door of the inn, leaving him to shuttle bowls to the retreat participants.

It was Francine. She was no longer soaked in soy milk but still looked madder than a wet hen.

"Hi, Francine. What can I do for you?"

"Where is your husband?"

"He's busy right now," I told her.

"I need to see him."

I really wanted her to cool off for a bit—maybe overnight—but I could tell by the set of her jaw that that wasn't going to happen. "If you'll wait here, I'll see if I can grab him," I told her, gesturing to the bench in the front hall as I scurried back to the dining room.

John was serving a bowl of fresh berries to Willow when I walked into the dining room and touched his arm. "What's up?" he asked.

"Francine's in the front hall looking for you," I said in a quiet voice. "She doesn't look happy."

His own eyebrows shot up. "Tell her I'll be right there," he answered, but he didn't have a chance. Francine, as usual, had taken matters into her own hands.

"I hear you're the island deputy," she trumpeted. The dining room went silent, and all eyes turned to Francine. "I want to press charges against the woman who assaulted me."

CHAPTER THREE

JOHN PUT DOWN THE BOWL of berries and let out a sigh. "Unless it's an emergency, I'm not on duty at the moment, Ms. Hodges."

"It *is* an emergency," she said. "I was assaulted."

I scanned the room, wondering how this unusual version of dinner entertainment was going over.

"Assaulted?" Kellie asked, her eyes wide. "I thought this island was supposed to be safe."

"It was soy milk," I said. "Not usually a lethal weapon."

As I spoke, Francine glanced around the room. Her eyes widened briefly, in something like recognition, but the flash was gone as soon as it appeared. "I can see you're busy," she said shortly. "I'll come by tomorrow."

John nodded. "That would be best."

But she'd already turned around and headed for the front door.

"What the heck was that all about?" Kellie asked. "Is it an emergency or isn't it?"

"It's not," I told her. "It was just a tiff at the general store... it happened hours ago, and everyone is fine." I smiled at her. "How's the sorbet?"

"It's not chocolate, but it's pretty good anyway,"

she replied.

"Chocolate's tomorrow," I told her.

"I don't know if I can wait that long," Blue, one of the three Texas women at the retreat, said. "What was the tiff about anyway?"

"Island beautification, if you'll believe it."

"Wow," Blue said. "I guess when you live on a small island, you have to make your own drama."

I grinned. "Something like that."

"How's everyone feeling?" Sequoia said brightly, drawing everyone's attention. "Ready for one last session?"

The response was lackluster. My eyes darted to Ravi; he was sitting in the corner with his arms crossed.

"After I finish this," Kellie said. "Thanks so much, Ravi, for helping me out with that pressure point." She arched her back, pointing her chest in his direction. "My back is so much better!"

"I'm glad," Ravi said with a small smile, then averted his eyes as Rainy glowered at him. Sebastian and Gage, I noticed, were conferring in the corner; Sebastian looked unhappy, and Gage was swinging one leg in what looked like irritation. His eyes, I noticed, flicked to James more than once.

"All right, everyone," Willow announced. "Fifteen-minute break, and then meet us on the back lawn for our sunset session. It'll smooth things right over!"

From the look Rainy flashed Ravi, I was guessing she was being optimistic, but I wasn't about to argue. I gathered the few empty bowls and hightailed it to the kitchen just as Charlene's truck bumped down the driveway.

A moment later, she exploded into the kitchen in a blur of rainbow-colored spandex. "Am I too late for the yoga session?" she asked breathlessly.

"They just went out to the backyard," I told her.

"Guess who's coming to visit?" she asked, eyes sparkling.

"The tooth fairy?"

"No, you nut. Only my favorite naturalist in the world."

Alex. "That's awesome, Charlene. When does he get here?"

"Tomorrow," she told me. "He just called to surprise me tonight!" My friend was absolutely giddy. "But I've got to run... don't want to miss tree pose, or whatever it is."

"When you get back, we need to talk; Francine stopped by earlier. She wants to press charges."

Charlene rolled her eyes. "I wish she'd just go back to Florida."

"You and me both," I said.

"And about half the island, too," she said dolefully.

"Well, that went well," John said when we climbed into bed, exhausted, at nine o'clock. Biscuit and Smudge, our two cats, deposited themselves between us, creating what we called the "wall of cat." Despite not getting along at first, they'd become fast friends; in fact, Biscuit had taken on the role of Smudge's protector.

I reached over and stroked Smudge's head, and she started purring. "Are you kidding me? You could have cut the tension with a butter knife."

"I know," he said. "I talked with Willow about maybe getting everyone outside into separate groups tomorrow. There's a lot of tension."

"And romantic intrigue, from what I can see."

"Thank goodness we don't need to deal with that," John said.

"I hope not anyway. Kellie was giving you the eye tonight, I noticed."

"She's more interested in James, I think," he said. "And Ravi."

"Where's Ravi sleeping tonight anyway? He didn't come to ask me about a room."

"I don't know," he replied, "but he must have worked something out."

"Either that, or he's pitching a tent on the lawn," I said.

"Can you imagine what Francine would say about that?" John asked, rolling his eyes.

"I'm sure we'll know by tomorrow morning," I said. "Hey... have you heard anything from Gwen, by the way?"

"She called earlier and said she'd be back late tonight."

"Is she going to have time to help out the next few days?"

"She'll be around a bit tomorrow afternoon, but she's superbusy."

"We're going to have to work something out. With a full inn, you and I can't do all of it and stay sane. Catherine's hardly been here either," I said, referring to his mother.

"She's been sailing with Murray this week, but she promised she'd be back by the weekend." Not long after moving into the carriage house behind the inn, my mother-in-law had embarked on a rather surprising romance with Murray Selfridge, one of my least favorite islanders. They'd been going steady for quite some time. He seemed to be completely enamored of her, and she seemed happy, though, so I kept my opinions of Murray to myself. Besides, she seemed to have had a bit of a softening effect on him.

"Everyone's busy," John remarked. "So much for quiet island life."

We had settled in and I was starting to doze off when a door slammed downstairs. I jerked awake.

"Think that's Gwen?"

He and I both waited for the sound of her footsteps on the stairs, but they didn't happen. After a moment, I got up and put on my bathrobe, then padded downstairs.

The kitchen was empty, and there was no sign of Gwen. I pushed through the swinging door into the dining room. There was a flashlight shining in the backyard, heading away from the inn. Was someone out for a late-night walk? I wondered. I stepped into the parlor and turned on the light. Someone sat straight upright on the couch, and I stifled a scream.

It was Ravi. His suitcase was next to him, with his toothbrush sitting on top of it.

"What are you doing here?" I asked.

"Rainy kicked me out," he said.

"You can't sleep on the couch," I said.

He spread his hands. "Where else am I going to go?"

"I'd book you into another room, but I'm afraid the inn is full."

"What's wrong with the couch?"

"It's my living room," I said. "It's a common area. People can't sit down here if you're bunking on the couch."

He was undeterred. "No one is up at this time of night."

I sighed. "That's not the point." I looked at Ravi. In truth, there really wasn't anywhere else he could go; the mail boat wouldn't run until morning, and there were no other inns on the island. "Look," I said. "you can stay here tonight, but I need you up and off the couch by six, and you've got to make other arrangements for tomorrow."

"I knew Willow shouldn't have had the retreat here," he said. "This island is so small, it's limiting."

"You're welcome to leave now if you'd like," I said tartly.

"We both know I can't, unless I swim."

"Fine, then," I said. "Let's make the best of it." I turned and saw a flashlight bobbing in the distance; as I watched, it winked out, probably hidden behind a boulder. "Did someone go out for a walk?"

"I heard someone go out the front door," he said, "but I didn't see who it was."

"Has anyone else come in?" I asked, wondering if Gwen had come back.

"Not that I know of," he said, and lay back down on my couch. "Do you mind turning off the light?"

"You're kidding me, right?"

"Sorry," he said. "I'm just... it's been a long day." As I stood there, he burst into tears. Which was just about the last thing I needed right then.

I stifled a sigh. "Do you need a drink or something?"

"I shouldn't, but... I'm having a hard time sleeping. Maybe a little something will help." He swiped at his eyes.

"The only things I've got are wine and tequila." The tequila had been a gift from my friend, Lucy Resnick, the last time she came up to visit from her farm in Texas.

His eyes lit up. "Tequila, please."

"I'll be back in a minute," I said, heading into the kitchen. I cut up a lime, grabbed the salt, and put them on a tray with the bottle of reposado tequila. The last thing I wanted was to knock back tequila with a jilted yoga instructor, but it felt like the right thing to do. Besides, I was hoping to see Gwen when she got home. I picked up the tray and went back into the parlor.

"This looks terrific," Ravi said as I set it down on the coffee table. "I love reposado." His hand darted out for the bottle, and he filled the shot glasses with expert ease, then squeezed a bit of lime on his hand.

"You look like you know what you're doing," I remarked as he sprinkled on some salt and then downed the shot, chasing it with the lime/salt combo.

"I used to be a bartender," he informed me as he poured me a shot and refilled his own. "Shall we toast?"

"To what?"

"To... greener pastures," he said, tossing back the second shot.

I took a sip of my own and put the glass down unfinished. "How did you get involved with the yoga retreat anyway?" I asked when he'd set down his empty shot glass and followed it up with a squeeze of lime.

"I fell in love with Rainy," he said. "She liked yoga, so I got in to it, too. She begged me to go to the retreat, and now that I'm here, she kicks me out. It just doesn't seem fair."

"How long have you two been together?"

"Two years," he replied, eyeing the tequila bottle. "But things haven't been great lately. I lost my job, and we've kind of moved in together. And she's really a lot more jealous than I realized."

"Does she have a reason to be?" I asked, thinking of his "trigger point" massage with Kellie.

He shrugged. "Maybe. The magic isn't quite what it used to be."

"But you still seem to care for her."

"I do," he said. "But... she's changed. She used to be about the yoga itself. Now it's more about branding, and money, and social media. She and Willow are talking about starting up a yoga channel on YouTube."

"I guess we all have to make a living," I said.

"Yes," he said. "But it's just... it feels different. Not genuine, you know?" He sighed. "I guess I thought coming here would kind of fix things between us, but I may be wrong. I probably just need to get a job and move out."

"You live in Florida, right?"

He nodded. "Rainy goes to Willow's studio."

"Do you have any idea why Willow and Sequoia picked Maine for the retreat?"

He gave me a look. "Have you ever been in Florida in August?"

"I'm from Texas," I told him. "I totally understand."

"Yeah," he said, reaching for the bottle and pouring himself yet another shot. "I drove up. It's pretty up here; maybe I won't go back. Maybe I'll just find a job here somewhere." He gave me a hopeful look. "Are you hiring?"

Although I was definitely in the market for more help around the inn, I wasn't sure Ravi was quite the right fit. I totally got the impetus to move to Maine, though; I'd taken the leap myself, and was still grateful I'd done it.

"Why don't you talk to Sequoia and see how the rest of the retreat goes?" I suggested.

"I don't have anywhere to stay," he pointed out.

"See how it goes today," I said. "I'll ask around on the island; maybe someone can rent you a room."

He was about to answer when there was a creak on the stairs; someone was coming down the steps. I turned to see Rainy, her eyes red from crying.

"Oh," she said, spotting me.

"I was just heading up to bed," I said, standing up and reaching for the tray with the tequila bottle. "I'll let you two talk."

"Thanks," she said as Ravi eyed her hopefully. He cast one last wistful glance at the tequila as I padded back to the kitchen. I was hoping they'd patch things up enough to at least get through the rest of the retreat.

I glanced at the clock in the kitchen; it was midnight, and I still hadn't heard from Gwen. I put up the tequila, then headed back upstairs to text her.

She didn't reply.

We often had a hard time getting phone service

on the island, so that wasn't unusual, but I was worried. As I climbed back into bed, John turned over. "What's going on?" he asked.

"I can't reach Gwen," I told him. "Should I call Adam?"

"She often spends the night over there," he said.

"But she usually tells us if she's not coming home." I bit my lip. "I don't know; I just have a bad feeling tonight."

He sighed. "Let's call Adam," he said. I picked up my phone and dialed.

He picked up on the third ring.

"I'm sorry to bother you," I said, "but is Gwen there?"

"She is," he said. "I'm just about to drive her home."

"Thanks," I said, feeling relief flood me. "I couldn't reach her, and I was worried."

"She dropped her phone off the mail boat today," he said. "We're going to the mainland to replace it tomorrow."

"Got it," I said. "Thanks so much. I'll be able to sleep now!"

"She'll be home in ten minutes," he promised. "I'll walk her in."

"Perfect," I said, and hung up.

"Everything good, then?" John asked as I plugged my phone in.

"He's driving her home shortly," I said, and closed my eyes. Ten minutes later, just as Adam had promised, I heard Gwen climb the stairs and slip into her room, which should have relaxed me enough to go to sleep. I tossed and turned, but sleep eluded me; something still felt wrong.

Unfortunately, it wasn't until the next day that I found out what it was.

＊   ＊

When I headed downstairs to start breakfast the next morning with Smudge in my wake, my couch was empty, and Ravi's suitcase was gone from the parlor. One crisis averted, I told myself as I headed to the kitchen and measured coffee into the grinder, inhaling the rich, nutty aroma as the little blades whirred. By the time the pot had finished brewing, I had whipped up the batter for a batch of Morning Glory muffins.

It was a quick recipe, fortunately, except for shredding carrots and chopping apples. It wasn't long before I poured the batter into muffin cups, sprinkled the dark batter with large-crystal Turbinado sugar, and then slid the pans into the oven. I quickly cut up a cantaloupe, then fixed myself a cup of coffee and headed out to the back porch to enjoy a bit of cool morning peace. Smudge, who had grown quite a bit since I rescued her earlier that summer, padded out onto the porch after me; I'd left Biscuit upstairs to snuggle with John.

Smudge jumped up onto my lap as soon as I sat down on my favorite rocking chair, and I stroked her silky head as I sipped my coffee. She'd gotten much bigger and healthier since I found her mewling under the porch, half-starved and only weeks old. She was just another of the good things that had come into my life since I moved to Cranberry Island.

I gazed out over the blue expanse of water behind the inn, and the craggy, ancient mountains of Mount Desert Island, the pink granite glowing in the morning light. Dark green trees blanketed the lower parts of the mountains, and a few wisps of mist played around the coastline, not yet burned off by the sun.

It was a beautiful view, and one that I greeted with delight every morning. Smudge kneaded my lap as I took another sip of coffee. I gazed out at the multicolored buoys studding the water; the thrum of a lobster boat's motor reached my ears, growing louder as it came closer. I waited for the sound of an idling motor as the boat's captain stopped to check a trap, but the motor didn't pause. I squinted as the white boat came into view, trying to make out the buoy on the bow. Once I spotted it, I didn't need to see the name on the back of the boat to know who was captaining.

I stood up and waved, expecting Adam to wave back, but instead, he turned toward the inn's dock. I put down my coffee cup and walked down to greet him as he tied up the lobster boat.

"Good morning!" I called out. "I just made a pot of coffee... want a cup?"

"I'd love to, but probably not now." He ran a hand through his dark hair. "Is John around?"

"He's still asleep. What's up?"

"There's a body down by the co-op," he said.

"What?" My heart raced. "Who is it?"

"Francine Hodges," he said. "Somebody bashed her in the head with a brick."

CHAPTER FOUR

ADAM WAITED IN THE KITCHEN while I raced up the stairs, Smudge at my heels.

"John!"

Biscuit glared at me as John sat up, looking bleary. "What's wrong?" he asked, rubbing the sleep from his eyes.

"Someone killed Francine Hodges last night. Adam found her by the co-op; whoever did it used a brick."

John winced. "Ouch. So much for the peaceful life on a small island." As he stood up and headed to the sink, Biscuit moved to the warm spot he had vacated. "Would you mind calling the mainland for me while I throw on some clothes? Tell Adam I'll be right down."

"Sure. I'll fix your coffee to go," I offered.

He smiled. "Thanks."

I poured coffee into travel mugs for both Adam and John when I got back to the kitchen. "Who found her?" I asked.

"I did," Adam said. "Ironically, I was loading up on bait when I spotted her."

"If you hadn't seen the brick, I might have thought she had a heart attack from the smell.

Where was she?"

"She was on the rocky beach a few yards from the dock," he said. "If she hadn't been wearing a yellow jacket, I probably wouldn't have seen her. It's a good thing the tide didn't take her out."

I handed Adam a mug, then reached for the phone and called the police on the mainland. It only took a minute to relay the information. As I hung up, there was the sound of footsteps on the stairs; a moment later, Gwen appeared, her dark hair a tangled halo around her pale face. "What's going on?" she asked.

"Someone did in Francine," Adam said, crossing the kitchen and giving her a hug. "I'm glad I made sure you got home safe last night. No more wandering around at night on your own, my love."

"Did her in? How?"

As Adam filled her in, John came down the stairs, dressed in jeans and a faded Cranberry Island Lobster Co-op T-shirt. He came over and kissed me, and I handed him his travel mug. "Thanks," he said, and turned to Adam. "Ready?"

"Why don't you go with them, Aunt Nat?" Gwen offered. "I'll take care of breakfast; it's the least I can do."

"Are you sure?" I asked. "That would be great."

"Positive," she told me.

"Muffins are in the oven, I cut up a cantaloupe and put it in the fridge, and the recipes for everything else are over there," I told her. "I'll take my phone."

"Mine's gone, but I can reach you from the landline if I need to," Gwen said.

"Thanks," I told her, and transferred my own

half-drunk coffee to a travel mug. "Nothing like a morning cruise to start the day off right, eh?"

"Too bad Francine is the highlight of the tour," John said, grimacing. "Or what's left of her anyway. Did you get through to the mainland?" he asked me.

"They're sending someone out this morning," I told him as he opened the door to the back porch for me.

"Why don't you join Adam on the *Carpe Diem*, and I'll follow in my skiff?" John suggested.

"Sounds good to me," I said. Adam leaped to the deck of the *Carpe Diem* and offered me a hand. Less than a minute later, we were motoring toward the lobster co-op... and what was left of Francine.

I sipped my coffee as the lobster boat cut through the dark blue water. The boat made the buoys on either side bob as we passed, and the wake looked like pearls of foam. A breeze came from the direction of the island; I caught a whiff of beach roses and the kelp scent of low tide mixed with the cool, clean smell of salt water. The mist on the mainland was already thinner, and the sun had risen higher in the sky; it was going to be a beautiful Maine morning.

But Francine wouldn't get to see it.

Who had killed her, and why? I wondered as we rounded one of Cranberry Island's rocky points and the co-op came into view. She and Claudette had certainly had it out the day before; I found myself grateful no one had seen it but Charlene and me. And Pauline, now that I thought of it. And everyone at the yoga retreat had known she was going to file charges for assault, I realized with a sinking heart. Surely no one would think Claudette killed Francine because she threatened her goats. At least I hoped not.

A few people were crowded on the beach not far from the co-op. There was a flash of yellow among the green-brown of the rocks and the black rubber boots of the lobstermen.

Adam docked efficiently, with John not far behind him, and soon we joined the huddle of lobstermen surveying Francine's remains.

"Looks like someone got fed up with the beautification committee," Gary Hall, one of the members of the co-op, remarked as John stooped and put a finger on where Francine's pulse would have been if her heart was still beating. There was a look of surprise mingled with outrage on her pale face, but something about the way her body lay on the beach, arms akimbo, made me think of a doll that had been flung aside. The water was lapping at her fingers, making her left hand bob up and down with the waves, and I turned away. I hadn't liked her, but it was upsetting to see this woman, who had been so full of energy and passion just the day before, with the life snuffed out of her.

"Where'd they get a brick?" Gary asked.

"It's got barnacles on it," Adam said. "Looks like it came out of one of the traps." Old bricks were often used to weight lobster traps on the island.

"Or just washed ashore," Gary pointed out, indicating the few broken bricks scattered among the mussel shells and granite rocks on the beach.

"The forensics folks will tell us more," John said, standing up. "We need to stay away until they're here, so we don't contaminate the crime scene."

Gary took a puff of his cigarette; as he blew out a stream of smoke, ash drifted down to the body. Too late, I thought, grimacing.

"What's this?" I asked, pointing to something red and shiny in Francine's right hand, which was half-hidden under her yellow jacket.

Gary reached to grab it, but John warned him off. "Let's leave it for the investigators," he said. "Everyone into the co-op, please." I squinted at it; it looked like a grill lighter to me. What would she be doing walking around with a grill lighter? I wondered.

Reluctantly, they stepped away, Gary throwing down his cigarette butt and grinding it into the rocks with his boot. It was a good thing half of us had seen him do it, or it might have been considered evidence linking him to the scene, I thought, but I didn't say anything.

As they traipsed up the beach toward the co-op, grumbling, I heard the sound of goats bleating. Muffin and Pudge had come loose from their tire again, it seemed; the two were standing in the grassy field above the co-op, watching us with interest.

"What's that on Pudge's side?" John asked.

"She's hurt," I said. "I'll be right back; I'm going to go check on her."

"Be careful," John warned me.

"She won't hurt me."

"Maybe she won't hurt you, but she's a fan of jackets," he said. "She got the sleeve of my field jacket while I wasn't paying attention the other day."

Pudge hobbled over to me as I cooed to her. There was a streak of blood on her flank; in fact, it looked like it had been sliced open. "Poor baby," I said. "I need to call your mom."

As I pulled my cell phone out of my pocket and dialed Claudette, I examined Muffin, who was a bit more reticent. I couldn't see any marks on her, but Claudette would want to take a closer look to be sure.

Eli, Claudette's husband and the island's boat-wright, answered on the third ring. "Hello?"

"Hey, Eli... it's Nat. I'm down near the co-op."

"I heard about what happened," he said. "Sounds like a nasty business."

"How did you hear about it?" I asked.

"On the wireless," he answered. "Anyway, what can I do for you?"

"Muffin and Pudge appear to have gotten loose," I informed him. "Pudge is hurt; it looks like she cut herself."

"Cut herself?" Eli asked in an ominous voice. "Or maybe that woman tried to do her in before she died."

"I wouldn't bring that up if I were you," I suggested. "I'd like to keep Claudette out of the investigators' crosshairs."

"Maybe you're right," he said. "Although after what happened down at the store yesterday, I'm guessing that'll be a bit of a hard sell."

He had a point, but I still thought it was best not to throw more fuel on the fire. "Anyway," I told him, squinting at the long red gash on Pudge's flank, "she'll probably want to come and collect them, and take care of Pudge. The cut doesn't look deep, but she's limping a bit, and I don't want it to get infected."

"Claudie's down to Emmeline's this morning, but I'll give her a call and tell her to come collect them."

"Thanks," I said.

"How's the *Little Marian* holding up, by the way?"

I smiled. Eli had made my skiff for me, and always inquired after it as if it were a favorite grandchild. "She's doing great," I said. And speaking of grandchildren, I hadn't heard anything about Claudette and Eli's clan, who usually came up to visit for a few weeks in the summer. "I've been meaning to ask: are the grandkids coming up to visit you at all this summer?"

"They're heading up this week," he said with pride in his voice. "I'm hoping to take them out fishing, and maybe start on a skiff for them to use while they're here." Although Claudette's grandkids weren't Eli's biological grandchildren, it didn't make a whit of difference; he loved them fiercely, and from what I'd seen, they adored him in return. Who wouldn't, though? I would have loved to have Eli as a grandfather as a child. Heck; I still would.

"Well, hopefully we'll get all this sorted out by then," I said, looking over my shoulder as the sound of a thrumming motor reached my ears. The police launch was on its way.

"I hope so, too," he said. "I'll give Claudie a call; thanks for the heads-up."

"Of course," I said, as Pudge gave me a hard nudge and then grabbed the hem of my jacket with her teeth. John was right about her love affair with jackets, it seemed... and I was relieved that the cut on her side didn't seem to be putting a crimp in her style.

"And if you have any extra cookies," Eli said in a conspiratorial voice, "feel free to drop them by the store."

I laughed; Eli had a serious sugar habit, but Claudette didn't allow the stuff in their house, so I kept him supplied at the store. "I'll probably make a batch in the next day or two; I'll drop some by the store and tell Charlene to save some for you."

"Much obliged," Eli said. "And as always..."

"I won't mention it to Claudette," I finished for him.

It was almost ten o'clock by the time I made it back to the inn. I'd waited with Muffin and Pudge until Claudette came to collect them; she'd been concerned about the slash in Pudge's side.

"This looks intentional," she'd announced when she squatted down to examine the wound. "I'll bet it was that woman who did it."

"Francine?" I asked. "She's dead."

"I know that. But before she died. Maybe someone killed her because she was hurting my goats."

"Maybe," I allowed. "But she and Muffin were out on the loose; she could have scraped her side on a fence or something."

"It's an awfully clean cut," she pointed out, standing up and smoothing her tunic out over her long, broomstick skirt. Her hair was up in a white, braided bun, and her jaw was set and angry. Claudette was a good woman, but she wasn't someone I ever wanted to cross. "Good thing the mobile vet is due this week. I'm going to have to put some antibiotic on it in the meantime."

"Do goats wear cones of shame?" I asked.

"If she leaves it alone, she won't have to," Claudette cooed to Pudge. "Who's a good girl? Did you break free from your tire again?"

"How did they get loose, anyway?" I asked.

She sighed. "I never know."

"Well, they're not wearing collars at the moment," I pointed out. "Is it possible someone set them free?"

"Why would they do that?" Claudette asked, perplexed. "I'd love to let them run free, but people are way too uptight about their gardens."

If not wanting my window boxes mowed down to stubs and my rosebushes defoliated made me "way too uptight," I was okay with that label, but I just shrugged. "Well, let's just get them home and not talk too much about what happened, okay?"

She blinked at me. "Why?" Then her eyes drifted down to the group of investigators down at the co-op. "You don't think someone might think I did her in, do you?"

"Well, you were pretty handy with the soy milk and potatoes yesterday," I said.

"The potatoes were all Francine. Besides, nobody saw that. Except you, John, and Charlene anyway."

"And Pauline," I reminded her.

Claudette grimaced. "So everyone on the island knows by now."

"Maybe. At any rate, just keep a low profile, okay?"

"You don't think they'll arrest me, do you?" she asked, paling. "I've got the grandkids coming to town. What will they think if their grandma's in the hoosegow?"

I put a hand on her solid arm. "I'm sure it won't come to that. Just... let's take proper precautions, okay?"

"Like not jumping for joy that Francine Hodges is gone?"

I patted her arm. "That would be a good start."

John had stayed on at the investigation scene, so I walked back, hoping the exercise and clean air would dispel some of the dark cloud that had settled over me since Francine had been found. Gwen had just finished washing up the dishes when I walked into the kitchen.

"What's going on?" she asked as I refilled my coffee mug and reached into the cookie jar, only to discover we were out of cookies.

"We're trying to figure out who bashed Francine over the head with a brick," I said. "Right next to the co-op."

Gwen winced as she slid the last plate into the dishwasher. "Ouch. Any idea who it was?"

"I know lots of people who won't exactly be crying into their coffee over her loss," I replied as I added a dollop of sugar to my own coffee mug and reached for my recipe binder, "but I have no idea who did the deed."

As I flipped through my binder to the recipe for lemon cookies—one of Eli's favorites—my mother-in-law Catherine waltzed into the kitchen, looking (as usual) like she was ready for a society tea.

"Good morning, darlings!" she said, giving Gwen a kiss on the top of her head. Gwen's eyes widened, and she looked at me. I gave her a slight shrug.

"You're in a good mood this morning," I remarked.

"It's a beautiful day, the sun is shining, and I have a dinner date on a yacht... what could be better?"

"Murray's taking you out?"

She reached up and fingered her pearls. "Actually," she demurred, "it's with someone else."

I blinked. "You're going on a date with someone other than Murray Selfridge?"

She let out a light, tinkling laugh. "Did I say date? I meant dinner."

"Sounds like a date to me," I replied.

Gwen turned on the dishwasher and leaned against the counter. "So, does Murray know about this?"

Catherine shrugged. "I didn't mention it, no. Besides, Murray and I are... well, taking a break. Anyway, it's just a friendly outing."

I grabbed a bag of lemons from the fridge drawer and reached for the flour. What I was about to make was nowhere near gluten- or sugar-free, but I liked the recipe so much, I was happy I wouldn't have to share. Except with Eli. And Gwen. And John. And Catherine. And probably Adam, come to think of it.

Maybe a double batch would be in order. "So, who is this mystery man?" I asked as I popped a pound of butter in the microwave to soften and preheated the oven.

"Oh, just a gentleman I met in Northeast Harbor a few weeks ago," Catherine said, blushing.

"What's this gentleman's name?"

Before she could answer, there was a knock on

the kitchen door. It was Murray, carrying a bouquet of flowers.

CHAPTER FIVE

CATHERINE LOOKED AS IF SHE'D been caught with a hand in the cookie jar. It was quite possibly the first time I'd ever seen her nonplussed.

"Don't say anything!" she hissed as Gwen opened the door.

"Here you are!" Murray thrust the bouquet of beach roses and delphiniums toward her. "I knocked at the carriage house, but you weren't there." Catherine had moved into the carriage house John had lived in when I arrived on the island. It worked well overall, although to be honest, we could probably use a bit more space. I had kind of been hoping things with Murray would move on toward something more permanent so we could reclaim the little house, but it wasn't looking too hopeful at the moment.

"How did you get here?" I asked, peering past him; there was no sign of his Jaguar in the driveway.

"I sailed," he said. "There's a picnic lunch on board, with a bottle of Veuve Clicquot, if I can tempt you, my dear."

Catherine blinked and took the bouquet from Murray, twisting her pearls so tightly I was afraid the strand would break.

"I'd love to," she said, glancing at me, "but I really should help Natalie out today. I've been useless the last few days, and I know the inn is full."

Murray drooped visibly. "Are you sure?"

"How about tomorrow?" she suggested.

"Catherine, I forgot... I need to show you something in one of the rooms; I really need your opinion." I looked at Murray. "Hold on for a minute... we'll be back."

Catherine followed me out of the kitchen into the dining room. "What's going on?" she asked.

I shepherded her to the front desk, where we were out of earshot. "You're welcome to go with Murray today, you know," I said. "We've got it covered... you can take over tomorrow."

"That's kind of you," she said, "but... I'm not sure I want to."

"Just offering," I said.

"I understand. Now. Was there something you wanted to show me?"

"Not really," I admitted. "I just wanted to talk without Murray in the room."

"Now," she said, "I'll start with the downstairs rooms."

"Don't you want to wear something more... casual?" I asked, eyeing her slacks and cashmere sweater.

"This *is* casual," she said, looking down. "Although perhaps I should throw on an apron, just in case."

"Good idea," I said.

"Tell Murray I can't make it," she said.

"And the flowers?" I asked. Catherine was still

clutching them in her hand.

She thrust them at me. "Could you put them in a vase for me?" she asked, retreating toward the hallway. "I need to get working."

"The cleaning supplies are in the room off the kitchen," I pointed out. That was the opposite direction from the one in which she was heading.

"Well, I'll just start by making beds then," she said, and bolted down the hall, leaving me with a handful of thorny flowers and an unpleasant message to deliver.

I walked back to the kitchen, confused as to what had just happened. Catherine had been over the moon about Murray since they started dating several months before. And now, all of a sudden, they were taking a "break," she was off on an unofficial date on someone else's yacht, and he was turning up with roses, champagne, and something of a desperate look in his eye. What had happened between them?

"Where's Catherine?" Murray asked when I got back into the kitchen, holding the flowers gingerly. One of the roses had pricked my thumb.

"She can't make it today," I told him. "With the inn at capacity, we're swamped."

For a split second, he looked like someone had let all the air out of him. Then he puffed up his chest. "I should have arranged things first. That's the thing about Catherine; business is important to her," he said. "Besides, I've got a conference call with my accountant this afternoon. Anyway," he went on, swaggering to the door, "tell her to let me know when she's ready to collect on her rain check."

"Will do," I said as he let himself out the back door. I watched him from the window; as he walked, his shoulders sagged, and as he clambered aboard his sailboat, I saw him look sadly at the inn, as if hoping to catch a glimpse of Catherine from one of the windows.

"What was all that about?" Gwen asked.

"I don't know," I told her as I pulled a vase from the shelf above the cabinets and filled it with water, then arranged the flowers and washed my hands, making sure to clean the little puncture wound. If Catherine didn't want the flowers, I'd take them; the roses were already perfuming the kitchen with their winey scent. Although it did make me a little sad to look at them.

"Did Catherine say anything?"

I took the butter out of the microwave and dumped it into a bowl. "She didn't want to talk about it."

"Uh-oh," Gwen said. "Think she was swept off her feet by someone else, or is there something else going on?"

"I have a feeling it's more than just another suitor, somehow. Maybe John can find out."

"Catherine's a smart cookie; she'll figure things out. I never was overly fond of Murray anyway."

"I never thought I'd feel sorry for Murray Selfridge," I mused as I set the vase on the table, "but I do."

"He can take care of himself, Aunt Nat." Gwen glanced up at the clock. "I can't believe it's almost time for lunch. Think John'll be back in time to help out, or do you need a hand?"

"I'm making shrimp salad for lunch, and the

shrimp is already cooked, so I'm good," I told her. "Besides, I want to finish up these lemon cookies."

"Are they for the retreat, or us?"

"Us," I told her as I added sugar to the butter and turned on the mixer, then reached for the eggs. Once the sugar and butter were pale and creamy, I started adding the eggs one by one. "How's the wedding planning going, by the way?"

"Don't ask.," Gwen groaned. "I've been so slammed trying to get these prints together for the shop and helping out with painting workshops, I haven't even thought about it."

"Maybe once things settle down in the fall," I suggested. I zested and juiced two lemons, then added the zest and juice to the batter along with a dollop of vanilla.

"Maybe," Gwen said doubtfully. "I was hoping to get married in the fall, but apparently you're supposed to book things months, if not years, in advance."

"The church is booked?" I asked.

"Not the church. The caterers!"

"We can help with that," I offered as I mixed the dry ingredients into the creamy batter, turning the mixture into a soft dough. The oven had come to temperature and the kitchen smelled of lemon-vanilla deliciousness, mixed with a hint of rose from Murray's flowers.

"I want you to be a guest, not a caterer, Aunt Nat!"

"I can do both," I said. "Besides, it would be cheaper... that way, you two could save your money for something else. Like a house." Adam had rented a small house since moving to the island, but I knew they both hoped to buy a place of their own someday.

"I'll think about it," she said. "After I get these prints taken care of."

I grinned at her. "To think, your mom was worried you had your head in the clouds."

"I could use a little more time with my head in the clouds about now!"

"No kidding," I said, rolling the dough into little balls, lining them up on a baking sheet, and thinking of what I had to do between now and lunchtime. Once I got the cookies in the oven, I'd start on lunch preparations. I smiled at Gwen. "Thanks for all your help this morning. Have fun!"

"I'm just hoping I'll have a few minutes to sketch!" she said with a grimace before heading out for the day.

The lemon cookies were all iced, and Biscuit and Smudge were eyeing me hungrily when John walked into the kitchen.

I looked up from the shrimp salad I was putting together; my husband's tanned face was grim. "Any news?" I asked.

"Homicide for sure," he reported. "But that was pretty obvious. Not a lot of bricks falling out of the sky on Cranberry Island."

"What was the plastic thing she had in her hand?" I asked.

"It was a lighter, actually," he said, confirming my suspicion. "And she had a knife in her pocket."

"What was she doing with a lighter and a knife? Was she planning on lighting the co-op on fire or something?"

"It's a theory," he said. "Need a hand with anything?"

"I've got it," I told him. "Your mom is doing the rooms; help yourself to a cookie."

His green eyes lit up. "Lemon?"

I nodded. "'Just save a few for Eli. I promised I'd slip him some."

"I think he's going to need them," he said.

I chose to ignore the implications of that. "Why do you think she was carrying a lighter? Low-tech flashlight?"

John shrugged and bit into a cookie. "Maybe she was a closet smoker. These are amazing, by the way. Mind if I have another?"

"I made a double batch, so there are plenty." As I tore up some kale for the salad Sequoia and Willow had requested, I asked, "The police have any theories?"

"I think so, unfortunately."

I winced. "Claudette?"

"Pauline reported the food fight at the store. And someone mentioned that one of the goats looked injured."

I sighed. It had been too much to hope that the police wouldn't find out about what had happened at the store—or Pudge. "Have they questioned Claudette?"

"They were headed to the Whites' house when I left," he said as he filled a glass of water and sat down at the kitchen table.

I ripped the kale with fresh energy, wishing it was Pauline. "Great."

"Any news here?"

"Well, the romance between your mom and Murray appears to be on the rocks." I told him about Murray's appearance that morning... and Catherine's yacht date.

He groaned and reached for another cookie. "I thought life on an island was supposed to be idyllic and drama-free."

No sooner had the words left his mouth than Sequoia burst into the kitchen. "They're fighting on the lawn," she gasped. "Help!"

CHAPTER SIX

I LOOKED AT THE CATS, AND then at the shrimp salad. "You go," I told John. "Let me put this in the fridge." John followed Sequoia out to the back lawn; I could hear the yelling from the kitchen. I quickly wrapped up the salad and tucked it into the fridge, out of the cats' reach, then hurried out the back door.

What greeted me looked like some maniacal version of Twister, only with lots of spandex and multicolored yoga mats. Rainy had Kellie on the ground, one hand gripping the Texan by the hair, and despite Willow's efforts to separate them, it just wasn't happening.

"I told you to stay away from him, you..." The words that came next would have made a sailor blush.

"Rainy!" Ravi was wringing his hands—literally—from the sidelines. "There's nothing going on, I promise you!"

"Right," Rainy spat. "Do you think I'm an idiot? I know what you two are up to."

"I'm a married woman!" Kellie gurgled. She couldn't do much else, because Rainy was sitting on her head. Her face looked like a squashed plum.

"Like that matters," Rainy growled. Kellie turned a deeper shade of purple.

"Let's break it up," John said in his most author-itative voice. Rainy continued to put the pressure on Kellie, but when John gripped her shoulder, she released her hold, sat up, and burst into tears. "I'm sorry," she sobbed, and ran to the inn, slamming the door behind her.

Kellie lay prone for a moment, catching her breath, before propping herself up and adjusting her spandex top. "What is that woman's problem?"

"I'm guessing she's jealous," Blue suggested in a dry voice.

"You think?" Kellie asked, looking more than a little bit pleased with herself despite her faux-per-plexed expression. Her face was still mauve, and her blond hair was mussed.

"I'm so sorry that happened," Willow said in a soothing tone. "Are you okay?"

"My hair's messed up, and I think she tore my top a little," she said, pointing to a microtear in her neon sports bra, "but I think I'll be all right." Her eyes drifted to the hotel. "I don't want to be around her anymore, though." She looked at Ravi, who looked like he was hoping the earth would swallow him up. "No wonder you were thinking of breaking up with her."

I didn't think it was possible for Ravi to look more mortified, but I was wrong.

"Would you like to take a break and have some iced tea, or would you prefer to keep going?" I asked Willow, not sure how she wanted to proceed.

"What kind of tea?" Blue asked.

"Green, with mint."

"Lots of catechins," James pronounced. "And fat-burning, too. I want to continue the session, but hydration is important."

"Iced tea it is, then," I said. I'd made a big batch for the retreat; I was glad I'd prepared. "I'll put the pitchers out in the dining room, along with some snacks."

"Low-carb?" James asked.

"I'll have a variety of options," I said politely before heading into the house. "You're welcome to come in; I'll have everything out in about five minutes."

"I'll help," John volunteered, following me into the kitchen.

"I thought yoga retreats were supposed to be about relaxation and harmony," I commented as I retrieved the jugs of iced tea from the back of the fridge.

"I'm not sure everyone here is looking for relaxation and harmony," John replied as he retrieved a few pitchers from a cabinet and filled them with ice. "I get the impression Kellie enjoys a little drama."

"Where do you think Rainy went?" I asked. I hadn't seen her in the dining room or the parlor.

"Probably to her room," John said.

I groaned. "You know this means Ravi's going to try to camp out on the couch again tonight."

"There's always Kellie's room," he suggested.

"Isn't she rooming with Barbara Sue? I can't keep them all straight."

"There's always the chance it'll be Barbara Sue who ends up on the couch," he commented.

"You think?"

"I've spotted Kellie and Ravi together a few times now. They seem... intimate."

"That's what Rainy thinks, that's for sure." As John filled the pitchers with tea, I arranged a plate with an assortment of seaweed snacks, fruit, cheese cubes, and rice crackers. My eyes strayed to the cooling cookies. Was carbohydrate withdrawal part of the tension I was feeling at the retreat? "What do you think? Should I put out some cookies?"

"I thought those were for us! Don't you have anything else hidden in the cupboards?"

"Stale Cheese Nips," I told him. "And one package of emergency shortbread, but it's not enough to feed everyone, unfortunately."

He cocked an eyebrow at me. "You really think carbohydrates are going to smooth over a love triangle?"

"Chocolate would be better, but I'm saving the cake for tonight," I said.

"All right, I guess." He watched like a hawk as I laid out about half the cookies, and snagged one of the ones I had left. "These are amazing," he repeated through a mouthful of crumbs. "How many are you saving for Eli?"

"I'll make another batch. I promise."

"I hope so," he said as I put the cookies and the snacks on a tray.

"Ready?"

John grabbed the pitchers, and as we headed toward the dining room, the phone rang. He put down the pitchers and answered it, then mouthed *the detective.* I sighed and went out into the dining room alone.

"What are those?" James asked, jabbing a finger

at the plate of cookies.

"They're lemon cookies," I announced. "Dessert tonight is going to be gluten-free. Unfortunately, these aren't... still, I thought it might be nice to have some comfort food. There are rice cakes, too, if you can't have flour."

"Who would eat rice cakes when you've got these?" Blue asked, reaching for one of the cookies and pouring herself a glass of tea. "Mmm," she groaned. "I feel better already."

"I need one, too, after that," Kellie said. Her face had returned to a normal color, and she seemed none the worse for wear. She turned to Barbara Sue, and then me. "I still can't believe she did that to me. Should I report her to the police?"

I gave her a bland smile and didn't remind her that my husband was the island deputy. "I'm sure it will all work out," I said, and drifted back to the kitchen for the tea. As I picked up the pitchers, I glanced at John, who was listening intently to the detective on the other end of the phone and didn't look happy. My heart twisted a little in my chest; had they fingered Claudette? I put the thought aside as best I could and carried the tea into the dining room, where the yoga folks set upon it as if they'd been in the desert for a week.

"Has anyone seen Rainy?" I asked Willow in a soft voice, once everyone was settled. She had moved out of the dining room to near the front desk, and we took a few more steps until we were out of sight of the other guests.

She shook her head. "I don't know what's gotten into her."

I had some idea—I'd been cheated on myself—

but I drew the line at sitting on someone's head. Besides, if anyone deserved to be squashed, to my mind, it was Ravi; unless Kellie had held him at gunpoint, nobody had forced him into intimate trigger-point-massage time with a spandex-clad Texas belle. "How are you going to manage things during the rest of the retreat?"

She glanced toward the hallway leading to the guest rooms. "I'm going to have to talk to her, I suppose."

"It might not be a bad idea. It would be nice to make it through the week without another murder."

"Another murder?" she asked.

I grimaced. "I guess you haven't heard."

"What?"

"Francine Hodges—the woman who came by last night—was found next to the lobster co-op this morning."

Willow's eyes grew round, and her delicate nostrils flared. "Murdered? How do they know?"

"It's hard to hit yourself in the head with a brick."

"That's horrible. Is it some kind of serial killer?"

"I doubt it," I told her. "But it might be best to suggest the guests take precautions."

"Like having a buddy system," she said. "But wait. What if your buddy is the serial killer?"

So much for the powerful calming effects of yoga. "I doubt the murderer was one of the retreat members," I reassured her. But was I right? There had been an odd change in the air after Francine came to announce her desire to press charges, and she'd left in an awful hurry for someone so intent on pressing charges that she'd trundled all the way to the inn. Had she recognized someone at the retreat?

Or had someone recognized her?

"Maybe we tell them to stick to threes," Willow mused, tugging fretfully at one of her dark corkscrew curls.

"I wouldn't put Rainy, Ravi, and Kellie together," I advised.

"Probably best not," she agreed. "In fact, I don't think I want to put any of them together. I can't handle much more relationship drama." Her eyes welled up, and she swiped at them.

"Are you okay?" I asked quietly.

"I'm trying to be," she answered through a haze of tears. "James broke up with me a week ago."

"James?" I asked. "You mean, the James at the retreat?"

She nodded.

"Then why on earth is he here?"

She rolled her eyes. "You've met him. He paid for it, so he sees no point in not getting his money's worth."

"Oh, Willow. I had no idea... I'm so sorry." And I hadn't. James seemed so health-obsessed and completely self-contained, I couldn't imagine him having a relationship with anyone other than a juicer. "You've been holding up just great."

"On the outside, anyway. I should be over it," Willow sniffled. "After all, it's not like he's giving anyone 'trigger-point massages' or anything."

"Still." I reached out and squeezed her buff arm, then handed her a Kleenex from the tissue box I kept on the desk. "What happened?"

She thanked me and dabbed at her eyes. "He said

I was interfering with his work and fitness schedule. I think I may be the only woman in the world ever to be dropped for a fitness app." She let out a short, bitter laugh that came out almost as a gurgle.

"Why don't you let Sequoia take over more of the retreat so you can take care of yourself?" I suggested.

"I was thinking of doing that, but with the whole Rainy thing, I really can't abandon her that way."

"I understand. It's your business."

She nodded and took a deep breath, then wadded up the Kleenex and made her hand into a fist. "It's time for me to put on my big-girl pants." Her eyes crinkled into a smile; with her dark curls and moist eyes, for a moment, she looked more like a teenager than a grown woman.

"James was an idiot, by the way," I volunteered.

The crinkles around her eyes deepened, and she ducked her head. "Thanks. And thanks for listening." She took another deep breath, and the professional mask smoothed her features. "I'm going to have to tell everyone about the murder."

"I'll do it with you."

"Thanks," she said. "But first, I'd better go talk to Rainy."

"What are you going to tell her?"

"That if she pulls anything like that again, she's going to have to leave." Her eyes narrowed and her chin jutted out. "Without full pay."

"Good for you," I said, thinking that if Rainy did have to leave, at least it would keep Ravi off my sofa.

Willow rejoined me in the dining room as Blue was interrogating me about the amount of lemon zest in the cookies. "They're so tart... like lemon bars. Can I have the recipe?"

"Of course," I said, catching sight of Willow's curly head from the corner of my eye. She nodded, and I excused myself. "I'll print it up tonight," I told Blue.

"Thanks," she said, smiling. She wasn't at the table with Kellie and Barbara Sue, I noticed; the other two Texans were by the window, both on their phones. I wasn't sure how they were managing to get service—it was spotty—and hoped if they were, they weren't posting bad Yelp reviews.

As everyone chatted and sipped their tea, Willow grabbed a glass and tapped it with a spoon. At the sound, the room quieted.

"I have an unfortunate announcement to make," she began.

"What? Did Rainy assault someone else?" Kellie asked in a self-satisfied drawl. Her hair, I noticed, had been returned to its previous coiffed perfection, and she appeared to have reapplied her lipstick. Maybe that's what she had been doing with the phone: using it as a mirror.

"No," Willow said. "I haven't spoken with her yet, but I will. The news I have is that there's been a homicide on the island."

There was a collective intake of breath. James, for the first time, showed a flash of emotion: surprise? Concern? Not for the dead woman, I was sure, but for himself. And then the questions started tumbling out.

"Where?"

"Who?"

"Are we in danger?"

"It wasn't anyone associated with the retreat," Willow answered over the din of questions. "The victim was a local. The police are investigating, and they haven't indicated that there's any threat here at the inn." They hadn't indicated otherwise either, but I kept my mouth shut.

"Who was it?" Blue asked, looking more animated than I'd seen her the whole retreat.

"Francine Hodges," I answered. "The woman who stopped by here briefly last night."

"How did she die?" James asked.

"I'm not at liberty to say," I told him, even though everyone on the island would know the details by sundown, if they didn't already.

"Well, how are we supposed to know what to look out for if we don't know how she died?" Kellie asked.

"My advice is to find a buddy if you go anywhere away from the inn," Willow advised.

"What if our 'buddy' is the killer?" Sebastian asked, wringing his hands.

His partner, Gage, rolled his eyes. "Honestly, Seb. We've been together for five years. If I was going to kill you, don't you think I would have done it by now?"

Sebastian blushed, and a few people chuckled, breaking the tension.

"Anyway," Willow continued, "I'm sure it had nothing to do with anyone here. We can just be a little more cautious, and doubtless the police will have the perpetrator in custody soon. If you have any questions, Natalie here can help you," she said, handing the hot potato off to me, and sat down.

I would have spent the next hour saying "I don't know" if John hadn't rescued me by poking his head through the swinging door. "Nat," he said in a voice that filled me with dread.

"I'm coming," I said, and excused myself to the kitchen.

CHAPTER SEVEN

"WHAT IS IT?" I ASKED when the kitchen door had swung shut behind me.

"They're asking a lot of questions about Claudette," he said. "They know she was a suspect a few years ago; they're wondering if maybe she really is a killer. And of course Pauline told them about the food fight."

"Of course," I said. As I spoke, the phone rang. John reached for it; we both expected it to be the detective, but I recognized Charlene's voice.

"It's for you," he said, and handed me the phone.

She launched right into things. "You heard about Francine, I presume."

"Adam swung by this morning," I told her. "John and I went out to the scene."

"I heard someone smashed in her head with a brick," Charlene said. "Who would do something like that?"

"That's what I was hoping you could tell me," I replied, leaning against the wall. "Who was angry at her?"

"The whole lobster co-op, for starters. And Claudette, of course."

"I know. Pauline told the police all about the little dustup in the store, apparently. And someone or something hurt Pudge last night."

"Uh-oh," Charlene said, echoing my thoughts.

"So we need to figure out who else would have it in for her."

"I'll see what I can find out," she said. "Have they arrested her?"

"Not that I know of."

She sighed. "Maybe Alex will be able to help me out."

"What time is he getting in?" I asked. At least someone's romance was firing on all cylinders.

"I'm going to go meet him at the mail boat in just a few minutes," she said. "I know it's ridiculous, with everything that's happened, but all I can think of is what I should wear!"

"I think you'd look good in a burlap sack," I advised her.

"You're sweet," she told me. "Any more news?"

"Oh, lots of drama at the yoga retreat, but nothing related to Francine," I told her. "Any word on how Gus is taking things, by the way? I thought I'd drop by with some cookies later," I added, glancing at what was left of the lemon cookies I'd made. It might be time to make another batch.

"You mean dropping by for some interrogation, I'm guessing."

"Sympathy and gentle questions," I corrected her. "You know how good the police force is at arresting the wrong person. If anyone would know who she was feuding with, you'd think it would be her husband." As I spoke, I grabbed a Tupperware container from a drawer and started filling it with cookies.

"Well, let me know what you find out."

"Likewise," I told her. "And I'd love to have you and Alex over for coffee or dinner or something, once you're done catching up."

"We'll see," she said, a smile in her voice. "I may not want to share."

I grinned. "Ah, young love. Give me a call later, okay? I think I'm going to slip over to the Hodgeses' house."

I had just hung up the phone when Catherine walked in.

"Did you hear the news?" I asked.

"What news?"

"Someone killed Francine Hodges next to the co-op last night or early this morning," I informed her.

"Francine? That woman who just moved into the big house and was trying to turn the island into Disneyland?" she asked with disdain.

Her description reminded me of Murray Selfridge, but I didn't mention that. The bloom seemed to be off the rose in that relationship anyway; maybe she'd see him with clearer eyes now. And maybe, I thought darkly, without the mitigating influence of Catherine, he'd start trying to take over the island again.

Nothing I could do about it today, though. I fitted the lid on the Tupperware. "I'm going to go take Gus Hodges some cookies," I told her. "If you could help John out with lunch and take care of the rooms, I would be eternally grateful. I'm happy to take care of dinner, though."

"I'm on it," she said, giving me a curious look.

"But why are you in such a hurry to visit the bereaved husband?"

"I'm afraid the police may think Claudette did the deed. I'd rather see if we can come up with a few other options."

"You mean suspects?"

I nodded.

"I'll see what I can find out, too," she said. "Be careful. There's a murderer on this island somewhere."

"Thanks for reminding me," I said with a half-hearted smile, and headed for the door.

I hadn't been to the Hodges' house since they moved in, but I was familiar with the sprawling farmhouse-style building on the far side of the island. Whereas before it had been a bit overgrown with beach roses and tall grass, now the yard was neatly trimmed, and the beach roses had been replaced by a line of red roses and hydrangeas that lined the front of the freshly painted house. The formerly shingled roof was now galvanized metal, and a line of turquoise rocking chairs lined the white-trimmed porch. The whole spread was pretty, but felt sanitized.

Sonorous bells chimed somewhere inside as I pressed the doorbell. I was about to press it a second time when there was movement through the wavy glass of the sidelights. A moment later, the door creaked open, and Gus Hodges stood there, looking bewildered.

He blinked. "Can I help you?"

"I heard about Francine," I told him. "I'm so, so

sorry."

He blinked again. "Thank you," he murmured.

I proffered the Tupperware container. "I brought you some cookies. We can arrange dinners for a few weeks, while you're... adjusting."

He didn't take the cookies, but just stood there looking at me with mild brown eyes. Then, as if waking from a trance, he shook himself. "I'm sorry. It's just... it's been a lot. Please, come in."

I followed him into the house, which carried on the *Coastal Living* look from the outside. The interior was done in bleached wood floors and white walls, with a stunning view of the Gulf of Maine from the windows that stretched along the back of the house. A carefully curated selection of beach-related artwork—none as good as Gwen's, I was happy to note—graced the walls. The only bit of color in the room was from a blue and gray throw cushion on one of the white couches.

"Can I get you a cup of coffee?" he asked, leading me through the sterile decorator living room to the equally stark kitchen.

"Sure," I said as I levered myself onto one of the metal stools lined up next to the concrete kitchen island. The place was beautiful, but not comfortable. From the huge, unadorned windows to the featureless expanses of empty concrete countertop to the dearth of soft furnishings, the house felt a bit like a stage set, or a surgical theater. "Would you like me to put a few cookies on a plate?" I asked as he filled the coffeemaker—a Keurig—with water.

"Sure," he said, waving to a bank of stark white cabinets. "They're in there somewhere."

I opened a few cabinets until I found a stack of

predictably white plates, and took one out. As I arranged the frosted cookies on the plate, I asked, "Do you and Francine have any children, or family, nearby?"

He shook his head. "It's just... or, was just, the two of us." A spasm of something like pain crossed his face. "We never could have children. It was always a sore spot for her."

"I'm sorry," I said again. "You hadn't been on the island for very long. And for this to happen..."

He pushed the button on the coffeemaker, and brown liquid spurted into a cup. "Well, it's not a total surprise, is it? She had a knack for riling things up."

"Oh, really? How so?"

He sighed. "Lots of ways, but do you want an example? Where we used to live, she got a bee in her bonnet about paint colors in the neighborhood, and it... well, it kind of got out of hand."

I wasn't sure how an argument about paint colors could "get out of hand," but I was curious. "What happened?"

"It's a long story," he told me, handing me a coffee cup, "but one of the neighbors ended up painting her house dark purple."

"Purple?"

"And covered the garage door with yellow smiley faces." A ghost of a smile passed over his face. "I thought Francine was going to have a heart attack."

"What did she do?"

He shrugged. "There was nothing she *could* do. The HOA didn't specify paint colors, so..."

"That must have driven her crazy," I said. "Is that why you moved to Maine?"

"We didn't move," he pointed out as he made himself a cup of coffee. "We just acquired another mortgage. Do you take cream and sugar?"

"Both," I told him. "Thanks."

I doctored my coffee—it wasn't fabulous, but I hadn't come for the coffee—and reached for a cookie. "Would you like one?" I offered.

He waved it away. "I haven't been able to eat," he told me. "I don't know... maybe it's shock."

He did look haggard. Haunted, almost.

I added a spoonful of sugar to my coffee, along with a dollop of cream. "It must have been a terrible blow."

"It was," he said. "Francine always did make enemies fast, but I just... on an island like this, I wouldn't have expected anyone to do something so horrible." He looked around the kitchen. "She was so proud of how this place turned out... put so much time and thought into it. And she barely got to enjoy it." He paused and took a few deep breaths, trying to master his emotions.

"Did she feud with anyone in particular?" I asked when he'd gotten himself back together.

His eyes drifted to the mail sorter by the phone. "We did receive a few threatening notes. But I didn't think much of it."

"Threatening notes?" I asked.

"I'll show you," he said. As I munched on my cookie, he retrieved three postcards from a square basket by the phone and handed them to me.

Whoever had sent them favored Sharpies and block handwriting. The first card had been sent two weeks ago, according to the postmark, and was fairly straightforward: GO HOME.

"Nice, eh? Wait till you see the next one."

WE DON'T WANT YOU HERE. GO HOME OR ELSE.

"Friendly," I said drily.

"Not as friendly as the last one."

I drew in my breath as I read the last postcard: THIS IS YOUR FINAL WARNING. LEAVE OR DIE.

CHAPTER EIGHT

"WOW," I SAID. "WHEN DID you get this one?"

"It came two days ago," he said. "Someone spray-painted the back of the house last night, too."

"Any idea who?"

"Not a clue," he said.

I squinted at the postmark. All the cards had been sent in the last week, and the postmark said it had been sent from Bar Harbor, not Cranberry Island. I could understand why:; Charlene took in all the mail, so she'd know in a heartbeat who the sender was.

"The first one was sent seven days ago," I said, flipping through the cards. "Did anything happen that might have sparked this?"

He shook his head. "Nothing in particular. You know how she was, though," he said with a grimace.

"I know she wasn't a fan of the co-op," I said. "Who else was she having trouble with?"

"The woman with the goats," Gus said. "She found them munching on the roses down the lane, and read her the riot act last week. And then there was the head of the lobster co-op, of course."

"Tom Lockhart?"

"That's the one. He laughed when she suggested they move the co-op; she was angry at him for days."

"Where did she want to move it?"

"Oh, out near the lighthouse. She wanted the main pier to be for tourism, and the 'dirty work' to be done far away from everything."

"She wanted to move the dock to where the rocks are?"

"Her thinking was that it would be downwind of the rest of the island."

"Of course," I said. Forget logic. It was all about the aesthetics. "What did he say to her proposal?"

Gus sighed. "He told her you can't have a functioning dock without a harbor, and that if she was interested in the *Coastal Living* experience, she should have bought real estate in Kennebunkport."

He had a point. "I'll bet that went over well."

"It didn't." He sighed. "I loved Francine, but once she got an idea in her head, she was like a terrier with a bone."

I reached for another cookie. "She came by the inn last night. Did she say anything about that?"

He shook his head. "Not a word. Of course, I didn't see much of her last night. I took an Ambien at around nine and was down for the count until this morning."

"Was she home at all last night?"

"She was. She was fluffing the cushions in the living room when I went to bed. And when I woke up, she was gone."

"Did she come to bed?"

He shook his head. "When I woke up, her side

of the bed was untouched. That's when I started to worry. I called her, but she didn't answer."

"I'm sorry to keep asking questions like this... but had she called you, or left any messages? Maybe left a note to let you know where she was?"

"No," he said. "Like I told the police, I fell asleep, and then I woke up... and she was gone. No sign of her." He took a ragged breath. "And now I'll never see her again."

"I'm so sorry." He looked lost. "How long were you married?"

"Forty years." His eyes misted over, and it looked like he was replaying an old film in his head. "I know she was... difficult sometimes. But her heart was in the right place, and she was all I had, you know?"

I reached out to squeeze his shoulder; he didn't shrug me off.

"With her gone, I don't know if I'm coming or going. She used to leave me lists of things to do. This morning, I woke up, and the list wasn't there." He reached for a Kleenex and blew his nose loudly. "I'm sorry," he said. "It's okay," I said in a soothing voice. "When did you find out?"

"Just a few hours ago," he told me. "I knew something was wrong when I woke up late: seven thirty. I always make her breakfast in the morning. She wakes me up at six, and while she goes on patrol, I cook her oatmeal."

"Patrol?"

"Making sure there's no litter on the road," he clarified. "Anyway, I went out looking for her, but I didn't find her. Now I know why." He shuddered. "A brick. So uncivilized... and messy. She would have hated that."

I tried to blot out the image of Francine's dead body on the rocks next to the co-op. I took another sip of coffee, but it didn't help. "When you saw her last night, did she seem upset about anything?" I asked.

Gus bit his lip. "You know, now that you mention it, she was. She said something about the goats."

My heart sank. "What about them?"

"That if they even *looked* at her rosebushes, she'd be eating roast goat for Sunday dinner." His eyes widened. "You don't think the goat woman was the one who... who did that to her, do you?"

"No," I said quickly, looking down at the post-cards. Claudette might be capable of many things, but I couldn't imagine her smashing out anyone's brains with a brick. "I'd say whoever wrote these postcards is more likely. Did you tell the police about them?"

"I didn't think of it when they came by to tell me," he said, staring into the distance. "I guess... I guess I was just too shocked. I still feel numb; it's like it's not real, like she's going to walk in that door at any moment."

"Grief is funny that way."

"The postcards, though. I don't know why I didn't think of that. Do you think I should mention them to the police?"

Someone threatens you with death and you don't tell the police? I decided to give him the benefit of the doubt; he was probably in shock, after all. "Of course you should. They probably won't be able to get fingerprints. But maybe the police will be able to find out who sent them, or where they were bought."

"They're just average Maine postcards," he said. "Cadillac Mountain, the *Margaret Todd*... typical tourist sights. There's no way to know where they came from."

I flipped through the postcards again, studying the black ink as if it could tell me its secrets. "The police need to know about them. And you never know... they might be able to figure out where they came from."

"How would they do that?" Gus asked. "Could they find out who spray-painted our house, too?"

"It's possible," I said. "Maybe someone saw someone; I'll ask Charlene if anyone bought paint. What color was it?"

"Silver. Here, I'll show you." He stood up and led me to the French doors off the living room. A cool breeze swept off the water as we stepped onto the expansive back porch.

"Right there," he said, pointing to a loose scrawl on the freshly painted wood siding. It was jarring against the picture-perfect exterior.

I ran my fingers over the words—GO HOME— and looked at Gus. "Same as the postcards. The writing is a bit different, but that could be because it's spray paint instead of Sharpie. I'm so sorry this happened to you."

"To tell you the truth, we haven't felt particularly welcome here," he told me.

"I imagine not," I replied. "It can be a difficult transition for some folks." I'd received a few bits of hate mail in my time, too, now that I thought of it. "I think some of it may be getting used to what's here, instead of trying to recreate the outside world. Folks like the island the way it is." I tapped the postcard. "But that doesn't make things like this okay."

"Or what happened to poor Francine," he said, tearing up. "What am I going to do without her?"

I touched his arm and stayed with him while the wave of emotion passed. He took a deep breath and looked at me. "Who do you think would have done something like this?"

"I don't know," I said. "Someone who felt threatened, maybe. I don't know if whoever did this is the one who... who killed Francine, but it's certainly possible." I looked back at the words on the house. "Spray paint makes me think teenagers," I told him. "But most of our teenagers are pretty mild-mannered."

"She didn't argue with any teenagers. That I know of, anyway."

"Before I forget... did Francine say anything about seeing anyone she recognized at the inn?"

His forehead wrinkled. "At the inn?"

"Yesterday evening," I prompted.

"That's right; you told me that earlier. Why was she there again?"

"She wanted to talk to John," I said evasively.

"She didn't tell me anything about it. Why do you ask?"

"Just a feeling," I said. "You know, it's possible she might have known one of the guests."

"Are you thinking someone at your inn might have killed her?"

"It's unlikely, but you never know."

"What are their names?" he asked.

I recited the names of the guests, but Gus shook

his head. "None of them sound familiar, I'm afraid."

"Ah, well," I told him. "I know you don't have a lot of family around here, so if there's anything that would help you out, please let me know. I can organize dinners, company... whatever you need."

"That's kind of you," he said. "Let me get my bearings, and I'll think about it." He turned his coffee cup around in his hands, looking like a lost little boy. "What am I going to do with myself today?"

"You're welcome to come by the inn if you like. There are a ton of yoga people there, but my door is always open." In truth, I was hoping he would come because I wanted to know if he recognized anyone.

"I'll think about it," he said as we stood up and walked to the front door. "Thanks for coming by."

"Of course," I said, handing him a card with the inn's information on it. "Call if you need anything. I'll tell my husband about the cards... and the spray paint. Someone should be back out soon, I imagine."

"Thanks." The words came out almost as a whisper. He seemed to be going downhill fast.

"I'm so sorry," I told him again, pausing at the front door. "Are you sure you're okay here by yourself?"

He gave me a wan smile. "'That which does not kill us makes us stronger,' right?"

"That's what they say," I said, thinking that Francine had gotten the raw end of that deal.

"The investigators need to head back out to the

Hodges' place," I told John when I got back to the inn. The kitchen was tidied, and he was relaxing at the table with a cup of coffee and a small plate with half a cookie on it.

"Why?" he asked as he finished off the last of the cookie. I sighed, thinking I should have made a triple batch, after all, and told him what Gus had shared with me.

"Gus said Claudette is the only person he knows Francine was feuding with, but I don't see Claudette resorting to postcards and spray paint."

"Why didn't he say anything to the police this morning?" John asked as I grabbed my recipe binder and sat down at the table across from him.

"He said he must have been in shock," I told John as I leafed through until I found one of my favorite easy cookie recipes.

"Maybe," John mused. "Shock does do funny things to people."

I looked up from the binder. "You know, I didn't check on the retreat. I'm so caught up in what happened to Francine that I'm not taking care of business."

"Relax," he told me. "Gwen and Catherine are at the helm."

"Did Tom stop by with lobsters for tonight?"

"Not yet," he said, "but we still have a few hours to go."

"I'll give him a call in a few to make sure we're on the schedule. Any more romantic trouble?"

John gave me a reassuring smile. "It seems to have simmered down. Rainy hasn't left her room, and Ravi and Kellie are playing it cool. Unless there's another love triangle I don't know about, we should be fine."

"Speaking of love triangles, has Catherine said anything else about her new suitor?"

He sighed. "I get the feeling there's trouble in paradise. I never thought I'd say this, but it kind of makes me sad."

"I know. Murray was so much nicer with Catherine on his arm. Still," I said, "just because she's going out with someone else doesn't mean she's done with Murray. Maybe she was just spending time with a new friend."

"She chose to clean toilets rather than hang out with Murray," John replied, grimacing

at the flowers. "If you ask me, that doesn't bode well. I'll have to see if I can find out who this mysterious yacht owner is. It's not someone on the island."

"You could ask her," I suggested. As I spoke, the kitchen door swung open, and Catherine walked in with an armload of towels.

"Speak of the devil," John said.

"Pardon me?" she asked, peering at him over the mound of terry cloth.

"Let me help you with the towels, and then I'll interrogate you," John said with a grin.

"Thanks," Catherine said as he took half of them off her hands. They loaded the washer together as I pretended to look through my recipes.

"Now," she said once she'd started the washer and rinsed her hands, "I imagine you want to know about the man I'm going out with tonight, correct?"

"That was going to be the subject of my questions, yes."

She drew herself up and looked down her nose at him—quite a feat, because he was about a foot taller than she was. With her blond head craned back, she said tartly, "The answer is, I'm a grown woman and it's none of your business."

Before John could respond, she turned to me. "The rooms are all taken care of. I'll replace the towels and run the rest of these through. I won't be here for dinner," she continued, glancing at John, "but I can help with breakfast."

"Thanks," I said. "I appreciate your help."

"And I didn't mean to be nosy," John added.

She sniffed. "Yes, you did."

"I just want to make sure you're okay. I care about you."

"Thank you," she said. "But I don't want to talk about it."

John hesitated for a moment before speaking. "May I offer one word of advice?"

She sighed and rolled her eyes. "Do I have a choice?"

"All I want to say is this: If you break up with Murray, try to do it nicely. It's hard sharing an island with someone who hates you."

He had a point. It certainly hadn't worked out well for Francine, I thought, as Catherine sniffed again. As I watched, my mother-in-law strode out of the room, head held high, like a younger, svelter Queen Elizabeth. Only minus the tiara and plus a cashmere twinset.

I turned to John when the kitchen door had swung closed. "So much for island harmony. Is Mercury in retrograde, or something?"

"I have no idea, but if this is a 'peaceful' retreat,

I'm not sure yoga is the thing for me."

He had barely finished speaking when there was a knock on the swinging door to the kitchen.

"Come in!" I called.

It was Sequoia, looking worried.

"What's up?" I asked.

"I can't find Rainy."

CHAPTER NINE

JOHN STOOD UP, STILL HOLDING his coffee. "What do you mean, you can't find her?"

"Isn't she in her room?" I asked.

Sequoia shook her head. "The door was ajar when I knocked. I walked in, but she wasn't there."

"Maybe she's out for a walk?" I suggested.

"Maybe," Sequoia said doubtfully. "She was supposed to help lead the later session. Willow's running one now, so I can't talk to her, but I was wondering if she'd said anything to you, or if you'd seen her."

"I haven't, but I haven't been here," I said, and turned to John. "I think we should take a look around, just in case."

"I'm sure it's fine, but it's probably good just to be sure," he confirmed.

The yoga group appeared to be turning themselves into human pretzels outside on the lawn as we walked through the dining room. James made it look effortless, but a few of the other participants looked... well... I'll call it strained.

"Tough pose," John said as we walked by.

"She puts them through their paces," Sequoia confirmed.

Rainy's room was on the first floor, near the end. The door was ajar, but the lights were off. John nudged the door open and stepped inside.

"Rainy?" he called. Although the bed looked like it had been slept in at some point, there was no sign of her. The bathroom door was ajar. The shower was dry—no one had used it that morning and the towel hanging on a hook was no longer damp.

I had just gotten back to the kitchen when Tom Lockhart appeared at the door to the porch, carrying a large plastic crate.

"Dinner has arrived," he announced when I opened the door to let him into the kitchen. I could hear the lobsters shifting around inside the crate as he carried it into the kitchen. "Where do you want them?"

"In the laundry room would be perfect," I told him. As he set the crate down near the washer, Smudge tiptoed over to investigate, pawing at the air holes in the side. Even Biscuit hopped down from her favorite spot on the windowsill to check out the new arrival. "Thanks so much for dropping them off," I said. "Can I get you a cup of coffee?"

Tom grinned. "I wouldn't say no to that."

As I poured him a cup, I asked, "What do I owe you?"

"We'll settle up later," he told me as he sat down at the table.

"I'd offer you cookies, but they're all gone."

"Eli won't be happy about that."

"I know; I've got to make another batch. Hear

anything else about what happened to Francine?" I asked as he stood up.

"All I know is that Adam found her this morning," he said. "And that one of the detectives asked me a lot of questions."

"Uh-oh." I poured two mugs of coffee and joined him, sliding one across the table to him. "Why?"

"We tangled a few days back. Publicly."

"Claudette had some issues with her, too," I reminded him. "And I'm guessing you two weren't the only ones. She wasn't a particularly pleasant person."

"She and Ingrid Sorenson got into it, too," he said. "Francine was looking to see if she could get elected to the board of selectmen."

"There's no way she would have won."

"Maybe not, but she got under Ingrid's skin. Started talking about Ingrid's slacker son, and how her parenting style must be a sign of poor management."

I cringed. Ingrid had suffered enough over her son's addiction issues. It wasn't at all fair to lay that at her doorstep... much less use it as a campaign talking point. "What did Ingrid say?"

"I believe she told her to stick her island beautification plan where the sun doesn't shine," he said. "And then there's the plan for the lighthouse."

"The lighthouse?" I hadn't heard anything about the lighthouse since Matilda Jenkins took on renovating it for the Cranberry Island Museum a few years back. "I thought that project was on hold because of funding troubles."

"It was," he said. "Murray has some new plans for it, though."

"Like what?"

"Someone expressed interest in bidding on it and turning it into a restaurant," Tom told me. "Murray's investing in it and helping broker the deal."

"Wait. I thought she was trying to get the lobster co-op to move... why the lighthouse? It's awfully far from the pier."

"That's the thing. Murray and Francine were concocting a scheme to make the lighthouse the focal point of a new tourist landing. They were going to make the lighthouse a 'destination restaurant,' and create a tourist pier."

"I thought she just wanted to move the co-op!"

"When she realized that wasn't going to work, she came up with another plan instead."

"That would decimate the businesses at the pier," I said. "Spurrell's is having a hard enough time as it is." The lobster pound had lost its manager a few months back; family members were pitching in to make it work, but it had been rocky-going.

"Did you know the Hodges bought two of the properties adjacent to the lighthouse right before she bought her house?"

"I didn't know that. I guess she had this in mind all along, then."

"And Selfridge has agreed to invest funds, too."

"No wonder she was in to island beautification."

"Exactly," Tom said. "The irony is, people love Cranberry Island because it's a real place with real people... not a cookie-cutter, Disney-fied destination. And yet, when they come here, the first thing people do is try to make it like everywhere else."

"I hope the islanders don't think I've done that," I told him, feeling self-conscious.

"Not at all," Tom said. "The inn was already here. You just renovated it and made it a going concern again."

"Thanks," I said, relieved. "But you're right; this seems to be a battle we've had to fight almost every year." And Murray Selfridge was usually involved. Could his current project be the source of the discord with Catherine?

"You'd think being accessible only by ferry would help, but sometimes I think that makes people feel it's more 'exclusive.'" He sighed. "I want my kids to be able to raise their kids here someday, if they choose to."

"We'll just have to keep the school going," I said. Although islanders had to send their kids to Mount Desert Island for high school, the local school was a key element to keeping families like the Lockharts on Cranberry Island.

"The new teacher has been terrific," he said. "The boys love going to school since she came. I heard Claudette's grandkids were asking if they could live here and go to school, too."

"Wouldn't that be fabulous?" I asked. "And speaking of Claudette, I'm worried about her."

"I am, too. She seems like a natural suspect. But she's not the only one who had issues with Francine; like I said, she and Ingrid had it out, too."

"Does anyone else know about that?"

"Half the island, I reckon. They were both waiting for the mail boat when it happened."

This was both good and bad news. Good, in that Claudette wasn't the only person to have publicly had issues with Francine, but bad in that I didn't want anyone else on the island arrested either. I took a sip of coffee and leaned back in my chair. "Who else do you know that might have wanted her dead?"

"Half the co-op, to be honest. But I don't think anyone wanted it enough to do it themselves." He grimaced. "She'd been nosing around and asking a lot of questions lately."

"About what?"

"About who owned some of the rental properties she didn't like, for starters. And who was drinking too much, and dropping comments about how the selectmen weren't doing a very good job of keeping the school tidy. She went after Sara Bennett the other day for not doing a better job with the dress code at the school."

"School isn't in session now," I said.

"I know. The kids were on the playground, and one of the boys wasn't wearing a shirt."

"And Sara was supposed to do something about that?"

"Francine was kind of out there," Tom said. "What's more, I heard she was on the mainland chatting up business owners for her new pier."

"What about Island Artists?" I asked.

"I'm sure she'd be happy to have them," Tom said. "As long as they could afford the rent."

I sighed. "What was her motivation, do you think?"

"She wanted to put her mark on the place, I guess. And they put an awful lot of money into that house. I'm not sure they would have gotten the funds out of it if they sold. Her husband must be a very patient man."

"I saw him this morning," I told Tom. "He

seemed really shaken up... almost in shock. I'm not sure how he's going to function without Francine to organize his life."

"How long had they been married?"

"Forty years."

"Wow," Tom said, almost reverently. "Does he walk on water, too?"

I stifled a chuckle. "I don't know about that, but he does seem to be a nice man. We'll have to invite him over sometime once everything settles down."

"You think he'll stay?" Tom asked.

"I don't know. He's still got a place in Florida. I guess we'll find out if he comes back in the spring."

"We'll see. In the meantime, though, we should probably figure out who brained Francine with a brick."

"It wasn't me," Tom said.

"I didn't think it was. But it was someone. And I'm afraid if we don't find out who, the wrong person's going to end up in jail."

No sooner had the words left my mouth than John walked into the kitchen.

"Uh-oh," I said at the look on his face. "What is it?"

"They're taking Claudette in for questioning."

"Oh, no," I breathed. "Did you tell them about our missing yogi?"

"I did," he said. "But she hasn't been gone very long, and considering what happened earlier..." He shrugged.

"What happened?" Tom asked.

"Lovers' quarrel," I informed him.

"Ah," he said delicately. I knew he and his wife, Lorraine, had had one or two of those over the years. He finished his coffee and stood up. "I should probably get back to the co-op."

"Thanks for dropping the lobsters off... and say hi to Lorraine and the kids for me!"

"Will do," he said on his way out the back door.

"That certainly brought the conversation to a halt," John remarked as Tom hustled down the pathway to the dock.

"Yeah. I wonder how things are going with Lorraine." John grimaced. "Not as well as they could be, I have a feeling. I'm more worried about Claudette, though."

"Have you heard anything?" I asked. He shook his head. "Not a word."

"Does she have an alibi for last night?"

"She says she was home, asleep."

"Eli was there, right?"

"He was," John confirmed. "But she and Eli have been sleeping in different rooms lately."

"Oh, no," I groaned. "More lovers' quarrels?"

"No," John said. "Claudette's CPAP broke, and she snores. She's sleeping in the guest room and waiting for a replacement part."

I sighed. "Figures. The one time she needs an alibi." I thought of the light I'd seen the night before, not far from the inn. "Is there an estimated time of death?"

"She was cold when I got there, so I'm guessing it was late last night."

"I talked with her husband; evidently, she came home before she was murdered. He said he went to sleep before she did, and when he woke up, she was gone."

"How upset did he seem?"

"I'm not sure. He just looked... shell-shocked. I got the feeling he's going to have a hard time figuring out what to do each day without Francine telling him."

"I'm sure he'll adjust," John said dryly.

"They were married for forty years."

"Think we'll still like each other after forty years?"

"We've made it this far," I said, walking up to him and giving him a hug.

"I like our odds." He put his chin on my head and gave me a squeeze. "I know dinner's lobster. What sides are you planning?"

"Coleslaw, corn, and boiled potatoes."

"Carbs, eh?"

"No flour or sugar, at least."

"True. Sounds like it won't take long. Have time for a walk?"

"Probably not," I said, "but it's a gorgeous day, and after everything that's happened, I could use a break; besides, I need to fill you in on what Tom told me."

"That sounds ominous."

"Did you know that Francine had plans for the lighthouse?" I asked as I grabbed a windbreaker from its hook by the door.

"Matilda mentioned she'd asked about it," he said, "but that's all I know."

"I'll fill you in while we walk," I said. I slipped on my shoes, and a minute later, we let ourselves out the back door of the inn.

It was a beautiful day, with a cool wind off the water. The tide had come in, and the mingled scents of salt, beach roses, and balsam fir was like the best perfume in the world. As we headed toward the little trail that followed the coastline, I looked back with pride and gratitude at the inn. The gray-shingled building with blue shutters and overflowing window boxes looked like it belonged on a postcard; sometimes I still couldn't believe it was mine. I reached out and squeezed John's hand. He turned and grinned at me, the sun glancing off his sandy blond hair. Life had been good to me, I reflected.

"Tell me what's going on," John said as we headed up the hill beside the inn. "But first, where are all the yoga folks?" The lawn behind the inn was empty of people in uncomfortable postures.

"They must have gone out for a nature walk," I replied. "I remember Willow telling me that was on the schedule. It's a beautiful day for it. Maybe a walk in nature will help chill everyone out."

"Here's hoping," he said. As we climbed the hill beside the inn, I told him what Tom had relayed to me.

"So, we've got another would-be developer on the island," he said with a sigh.

"And Murray's involved again. I'm wondering if that's what's going on with Catherine."

"I'll find out soon enough, I'm sure."

As we climbed over the crest of the hill, I spotted the *Island Queen* chugging toward the island.

"Alex van der Berg is here to visit, by the way," I informed John. "I forgot to tell you."

"The naturalist from the tour that was on the island a while back? Charlene's beau?" he asked.

"The same," I replied.

"Does he know about her dating track record?"

"Why should he?" I asked. "It's not like she had

anything to do with what happened to them." I squinted at the boat, hoping Alex had indeed made it over to the island... and that things for at least one couple would go well.

"Natalie." John's tone of voice stopped me in my tracks.

I turned to him. "What is it?"

"I found Rainy," he said, pointing to a crumpled figure on the path in front of us.

CHAPTER TEN

MY HEART CLENCHED IN MY chest as we hurried over to her. John put his fingers on her neck to look for a pulse, and I put a hand on her chest, hoping she was still breathing. To my relief, her chest rose almost imperceptibly. "She's alive."

"She is, but she doesn't look good." John was right; her color was pale.

"Any sign of trauma?" I asked. In Rainy's right hand was a flashlight. Was she the person I'd seen out walking the cliffs last night? And if so, what had happened to her?

"Nothing I can see, anyway," John answered. "Did you think to bring your phone?"

"No," I confessed. "I'll run back and call... I don't know if they still have police on the island, but what we need most is a paramedic, I think."

"I'll stay with her," John said, and I ran back to the inn. "Bring a blanket!" he called.

"I will," I promised as I jogged down the path, hoping Rainy would be okay.

The yoga group was filtering into the parlor when I burst into the inn a few minutes later, panting. "What's wrong?"

"We found Rainy," I told her. "I'm going to call for a paramedic... I'll be right back."

"Oh, no," Willow said. "What happened to her?"

"I don't know, but she's unconscious. I have no idea how long she's been there."

"I'm a paramedic," Sebastian announced.

"Thank goodness," I said. I had the feeling time was of the essence for Rainy. "Let me grab my phone and a blanket and you can follow me up there."

"I'm going too," Ravi announced.

"Actually," I hedged, "I think it would be best not to have a crowd."

"I'm her boyfriend!" he objected. "There's no way you're keeping me away from her."

I sighed. "Just keep your distance, then. It may be a crime scene."

Willow gave me a horrified look. "A crime scene?"

"I don't know anything yet," I told her. "But considering what happened last night..."

"I'll grab my kit," Sebastian said, and disappeared toward the guest rooms.

"I'll meet you here in a minute," I told him, and hurried into the kitchen to retrieve my phone. I grabbed a blanket from the laundry room while I was there, and hurried back out to where the participants of the yoga retreat were buzzing like an angry beehive.

By the time I got back to the parlor, there was an entire contingent of retreat participants clamoring to join us. I looked to Willow for help, but she just shrugged.

"Let's go," I told Sebastian, who was there with a

small black backpack. Together, we headed out the back door, with Willow, Ravi, Gage, and the Texas contingent in our wake.

"The police are on their way," I told John as Sebastian and I arrived, with half the yoga retreat following close behind.

"Oh, Rainy," Ravi said breathlessly. He tried to push past me, but I held him back. "Let's let Sebastian take a look at her first," I advised him.

"But..."

"I'll need some room," Sebastian informed him in a no-nonsense tone of voice. As I watched, he squatted down next to Rainy and examined her. "She's cold," he said as he checked her pulse. "Can I have the blanket?"

"Of course." I draped it over her prone form as he continued to work.

"What do you think?" John asked.

Sebastian looked up at Ravi, who was literally wringing his hands as he stood nearby. "Do you know if she was on any medications?"

Ravi shook his head. "I think she was on an antidepressant, but I don't know what kind."

"Anyone else know?" Sebastian asked.

Willow and Sequoia shook their heads. "She seemed healthy to us. She did take some supplements, but I don't know what kind."

"We should check her room and see what medications are in there," he said, looking at me. "Regardless, they'll want to know what's in her system."

"Are you thinking she might have overdosed?"

I asked.

"It's presenting as if that might be what's going on. Is someone on the way to take her to the hospital?"

"The hospital... oh, God..." Ravi moaned. It looked like he was on the verge of hyperventilating; Sebastian had his hands full.

"I called," I assured Sebastian as Willow moved next to Ravi and touched his arm, trying to calm him. I glanced at Kellie; she was examining her nails. As I watched, she leaned over and murmured something to Barbara Sue, who smirked and whispered a response. Nice.

"If you'll go check her room, Sebastian and I will stay with her," John said, refocusing my attention on Rainy.

"I'm on it," I told him. "Why don't you all come back with me?" I suggested to the group.

"Yes," Willow said. "I'd like to run everyone through a few poses before dinner to clear some of our chakras; it's been an energetically challenging day."

"I'm staying here," Ravi said in a petulant voice. He was still panting a bit.

"Why don't you come back with us?" Sequoia suggested. "Rainy's in good hands, and it looks like you could use some self-care right about now."

"But..."

"We've got her taken care of," John said in an authoritative voice. "There's nothing you can do here. Sebastian and I will make sure she gets the medical attention she needs."

"Besides," I said, "if you're sharing the room with Rainy, maybe you can help find her prescriptions for me."

"I hadn't thought of that," he replied, blinking.

"Come with us," Sequoia said, taking his arm and speaking gently. He resisted for a moment before following her, reminding me of a little lost lamb.

I walked back to the inn with the group, wondering what had happened to Rainy. Had she tried to commit suicide? That certainly seemed to be the opinion of Kellie, who was talking in a stage whisper loud enough that the whole group could hear her.

"I can't believe she OD'd," she was telling Blue and Barbara Sue. "I knew she was in to Ravi, but who tries to kill herself just because her boyfriend might like somebody else?"

I glanced at Ravi, but he was still wringing his hands, looking like he was in another world.

"Do you think that's what happened?" Barbara Sue asked in a gossipy tone.

"Let's see what the doctor says," Blue suggested, echoing my own thoughts. "We don't even know what's wrong with her; it's a little early to start theorizing about what she did or didn't do."

"I know she was jealous," Kellie said. "She told me I should be ashamed of myself because I was a married woman. Just for getting a massage!"

"She did?" Barbara Jean asked, in a tone that reminded me of a middle-school girl trying to win the favor of the queen bee. Which I was sure Kellie had been... and still was. "That's crazy," Barbara Jean continued.

"I know. Ashamed? For getting a massage? Please. If her boyfriend was happy with her, she wouldn't have to worry, anyway. I know my husband would never be with anyone else."

"I thought the same thing about my husband," offered Virginia.

Kelli looked at her. "What happened?"

"He ran off with his college sweetheart," she said. "I always thought he was devoted to me."

"You, too?" asked Andrew. "I just divorced six months ago for the same reason." He gave a wry chuckle. "And she always thought I was the one who was going to leave her."

"Do you have kids?" Virginia asked.

"Three," he told her. "The last one just went to college."

"That's a tough transition," Virginia said. As they spoke, the two drifted to the back of the group. I glanced over my shoulder; Kellie didn't look at all fazed.

"You know, Mike's been spending a lot of time at the office lately," Barbara Jean said. "Do you think maybe he could be having an affair?"

Kellie's eyes darted to the side for a moment. "Of course not. He's devoted to you."

"That's just what Virginia said," Barbara Jean said darkly.

She had a point, I thought as I opened the back door to the inn. As the yoga retreat members filed in behind me, I headed for the skeleton key hidden in a drawer of the front desk. Relationships could be hard, I reflected. I hoped the problems with Ravi hadn't been enough to send Rainy over the edge.

Ravi followed me up the stairs, and together we

entered Rainy's room. There was a suitcase piled with brightly colored yoga clothes in one corner, and Ravi's smaller, zipped-up suitcase was tucked neatly next to the wardrobe; I couldn't remember if it had been there earlier. Had Ravi spent the night here? I wondered. Or had he paid a visit to Kellie? The vanity on the sink looked like someone had shoplifted every sample from the Whole Foods beauty aisle and dumped them out on the counter. I didn't see any prescription bottles, but there were at least three supplement bottles mixed in with the creams and lip balms.

"Do you know if she has any prescriptions?" I asked Ravi as I looked at the labels, which purported to contain turmeric, Gingko biloba, and a proprietary mood-lifting formula. Was it possible to OD on supplements?

"I think so," he said. "They might be in her suitcase."

I knelt next to the suitcase and checked the outer compartments. There was a pair of shoes, but no medications. The interior of the suitcase was a jumble of clothing, but again, no bottles. As I searched the suitcase, Ravi opened Rainy's nightstand drawer.

"Here," he said, holding up an orange prescription bottle. "Klonopin. I think she took it for anxiety."

"That might have caused issues," I said; I'd heard Klonopin was one of the drugs that people sometimes got addicted to. And with everything going on with Ravi, I was guessing anxiety had been an issue the last few days.

"Do you know if she took any last night?"

He shook his head, and looked away.

"Ravi," I said. "Did you two argue again last night?"

He darted his eyes at me, then burst into tears. "I hate myself," he said. "She loves me so much, and I'm... I'm just such a bad person." He swiped at his eyes.

"What happened?" I asked in my gentlest voice.

"She asked about Kellie," he said. "And... I was honest. Big mistake."

I wasn't sure the "big mistake" was being honest, but I said nothing.

"I kissed her," he confessed. "I shouldn't have, but the moment was there, and then she just kind of went for it." He looked up at me, miserable. "I never should have agreed to give her that massage."

"What happened when you told her?"

"She took a pill," he confessed, nodding to the little orange bottle, "and then she took a flashlight and said she needed to go out for a while. Only... she never came back."

"Are you sure it was just one pill?" And why hadn't he told me about it in the first place?

"I don't know," he said. "I wasn't paying attention to that. I was too busy begging her to forgive me."

"What time did she leave?" I asked.

"Around eleven," he said. "We'd just... we'd argued, like I said. She said she had to think about things."

"Why didn't you tell someone she hadn't come back when you got up this morning?" I asked.

"I... I was embarrassed," he said. For a man of around twenty-five, he seemed more like a five-year-old in many ways. If Rainy survived, which

I fervently hoped she did, she might be better off without him.

"Can I see the bottle?" I asked. He handed it to me. Although the label said she'd had a thirty-day supply filled just last week, it looked like more than half the bottle was gone. I had a bad feeling about this.

"We've got to get this to Sebastian. Any other prescriptions?" I asked.

"Not that I know of," he said.

"Honest?"

He blinked. "Honest. I swear."

I grabbed the supplements and the prescription bottle and headed for the door. "Let's go, then," I said.

Rainy was still unconscious when I got back to the hillside. I'd convinced Ravi to stay back at the inn; I wanted a chance to talk with John alone.

"We found this," I said, handing Sebastian the bottle of Klonopin.

He squinted at the bottle. "This stuff can be addictive," he said.

"A lot of it seems to be gone. There were some supplements, too," I told him, handing him the bottles.

He scanned the labels. "Unless what's in the bottles is different from the labels, none of these supplements could have resulted in this, but the Klonopin could be an issue. Thanks for getting them."

"How's she doing?"

"Same," he reported. "But I found a contusion

on the back of her head. She might have hit it on a rock when she fell. They'll want to do a CAT scan, look for signs of internal bleeding."

Or someone might have hit her, I thought, thinking of what had happened to Francine.

"I hope they get here soon," I fretted, scanning the blue water.

As I spoke, there was a thrumming noise. I squinted at the sky.

"I think they'll be here momentarily," John said as a helicopter made a beeline for the island. Within minutes, it had landed on a knoll nearby and two women jumped out.

"How's Ravi?" John asked as Sebastian and the paramedics exchanged notes.

"I think he feels guilty," I told him, reporting what he'd told me about his interlude with Kellie. "He didn't tell me about the Klonopin at first, either. At first, he said he wasn't sure if she was on a prescription and suggested I look in her suitcase. A few minutes later, though, he 'found' the bottle in the night table, and then told me she'd taken one before she walked out."

"Do you think it's possible he slipped it to her?"

"That's what I was wondering. The bottle was supposed to be a thirty-day supply, but there aren't very many pills in it."

"Was he trying to kill her, or just trying to settle her down?"

"I don't know what he'd have to gain by killing her," I said. "If she does die, he's going to have an awfully heavy conscience, I think."

We watched as the paramedics loaded her into the copter and made their farewells to Sebastian.

As it lifted off, he brushed off his hands and walked over to us.

"How is she?" I asked as we watched the helicopter speed over to the mainland.

"We'll see," he said. "Any way to get in touch with her next of kin?"

"We'll ask Ravi and Willow when we get back," I told him. My heart sank at the thought of the unconscious young woman. I prayed she survived—and that she wasn't incapacitated by a brain injury.

We were just getting back to the inn when a sleek white yacht slid up to the dock.

"Who's that?" Sebastian asked.

"My mother's date," John said tersely.

"We don't know if it's a date," I pointed out feebly. As we watched, a handsome graying man tied up, then leaped lightly to the dock, a bouquet of exotic flowers in his hand. We watched as he knocked at Catherine's door. She opened the door, took the flowers, and disappeared inside, leaving him on the front step.

"Looks like a date to me," John said.

A moment later, she emerged and closed the carriage-house door behind her, looking summery and beautiful in a floral fit-and-flare dress and a springy green cardigan.

"Your mom's a good-looking woman," Sebastian commented. "Great style."

"I know," John said as the man took her arm and escorted her to the dock. As he helped her aboard, I saw another yacht purring by, a few hundred yards offshore.

It was Murray's.

CHAPTER ELEVEN

DINNER WAS STRAINED THAT NIGHT, to say the least.

"At least we have lobster," John said as we plated one of the pound-and-a-half shellfish Tom had dropped off earlier. I'd kept a few back for the lobster bisque I planned to make later in the week.

"Too bad we can't give them wine to go with it. Things are a bit tense out there."

"We do what we can," John said as I added some of my homemade slaw to each plate. "Ready?"

I finished up the last few plates and nodded. "Showtime."

Together, we ferried the cooked lobster out to the dining room.

Sebastian and Gage were huddled together by one of the windows, and on the other side of the room, the Texas trio whispered to one another. Ravi was in a corner, staring at a cell phone, while Sequoia and Willow talked in faux-chipper tones. The only comfortable pair was Virginia and Andrew, who had fallen into an easy companionship.

"Are weekends always this exciting?" Virginia asked when I set a plate down in front of her.

I smiled. "No, thank goodness."

"Ooh, this looks fabulous," she said. "I love fresh lobster; what a treat!"

"I'm almost more excited about the potatoes," Andrew replied. "Is that real butter on them?"

"It is. There's plenty more if you need it," I told him. "And flourless chocolate cake for dessert."

"That sounds amazing. Can I just move here permanently?" Virginia asked.

I grinned at her. "Why not? I did!"

She sighed and stole a glance at Andrew, then out at the panoramic view of Mount Desert Island. "Despite everything going on, this has been just magical."

"It has," Andrew agreed in a tone of voice that made me think they might be on the way to becoming more than friends. At least one romance on the island might be going well, I thought as I retreated to the kitchen for another few plates.

I had just finished refilling water glasses when the phone rang. It was Charlene.

"I heard you found another body," she said when I picked up.

"Not a body... at least I hope not."

"One of the yoga people, I hear. The whole island's talking about the helicopter. So far, the theories involve a Bigfoot attack, a fall from a cliff, and a lovers' quarrel."

"Well, they may be part right."

"Which part? Bigfoot?"

"Lovers' quarrel," I said. "Although it's looking like it might be an accidental overdose of some antianxiety medication."

"Poor thing," she said. "Although I totally get it."

"Maybe," I said. I suddenly realized she hadn't said

a word about her own romantic visitor. "Where's Alex, by the way?"

"Off on a lobster boat, taking pictures," she said in a surly tone of voice.

"What?"

"He's shooting the island for a magazine. I'm beginning to wonder if that's the only reason he came."

"I'm so sorry, Charlene."

"I should have known it was too good to be true. Maybe I'll just embrace the single life." She paused. "Or move to Portland."

I gripped the phone. "Portland? Why?"

"More eligible bachelors," she said. "I figure Tania could take over the store and I could get a job in a bookstore or something."

Charlene couldn't leave Cranberry Island. What would I do without her? "Why don't you start with an online dating service?" I suggested, trying not to sound desperate. "Maybe focusing on Mount Desert Island? If Alex is willing to fly across the country to be with you, I'm guessing there's no dearth of men on the mainland who'd be happy to take the ferry."

"Only he didn't fly across the country for me," she pointed out.

"You don't know that," I reminded her. "And even if that is the case, there are other fish in the sea. Closer ones."

She sighed. "I'll think about it. But I found two jobs I'm going to apply for. Just to see."

Maybe I should suggest she list me as a reference. I could say she was a horrible employee who had a thing for flinging potatoes at customers. Even if

was Francine who'd been doing the potato-fling-
ing. *Don't be selfish, Nat,* I chided myself.

"Come over tonight," I said. "I could use the
company."

"I'm supposed to have dinner with Alex," she
said. "But if he doesn't show by seven, I'm coming over." "When is dinner supposed to be?" "Who
knows? I'm not even sure when he'll be back."

"I've got flourless chocolate cake that needs eating. It's good for bad moods."

"You're tempting me."

"I'll even make Irish coffee if you ask nicely," I
offered.

"All right," she said.

"I'm here all night," I told her.

"Lots of cream in the coffee?"

"As much as you want," I promised.

🖋   🖋

"I almost forgot to tell you," Charlene said when
she'd finished her first piece of cake. Alex had been
"running late," and my friend was less than pleased
with him. She'd arrived at eight and allowed me to
ply her with chocolate and whiskey, both acces-
sorized with lavish amounts of cream. I hadn't been
able to talk her out of applying to jobs in Portland
yet, but I was hoping the second Irish coffee would
help. "Matilda came to the store in a tizzy today."

"What's going on?"

"Apparently, her lighthouse museum plans may
have been quashed. Ingrid just came over and
informed her that the board of selectmen is considering other uses for the building."

"I knew Francine was pushing for it, but Tom

didn't say anything about that going ahead," I replied. "What did she say?"

"That it's going to be a coffee shop/bookstore," Charlene said. "Which makes no sense at all. Who's going to walk all the way from the pier to the lighthouse?"

"Apparently, that's not the plan." I told her what I'd heard about the alternate pier.

Charlene sat up and waved her fork at me. "That would destroy all the businesses on the main pier!"

"Unless the merchants moved," I pointed out. "But I'm sure the rent will be exorbitant."

"How are they going to get people over there?"

"I don't know yet. Maybe they'll add a ferry stop."

"Or get rid of the existing one, more likely," she said. "What I want to know is, who's behind this?"

"Francine, from what I've heard."

"She can't do much to champion it now, but the damage may have already been done. And Murray, I'm guessing. He's wanted to develop this island since he set foot on it."

"Maybe when Catherine gets back from her date with the mystery yachter, we can ask."

"What?"

I filled Charlene in on what had happened earlier that day.

"Two bouquets of flowers in one day," Charlene said, looking at the vase of roses and delphiniums on the kitchen table. "Where am I going wrong?"

"I told you there were eligible bachelors here," I said.

"Yeah, but Murray Selfridge?" She lifted her Irish coffee to her lips, the door to the back opened, and

Catherine swept in, her cheeks pink as roses.

"We were just talking about you. Irish coffee?" I offered, lifting my glass mug.

"No, thanks." She perched on one of the kitchen chairs and touched her hair, which looked rather windblown. "I've already had half a bottle of champagne."

"How did your outing go?"

"It was wonderful," Catherine gushed. "Nicholas is such a gentleman. Champagne, lobster, sunset at sea... it was a perfect evening."

"How do you meet these amazing men?" Charlene asked, eyes wide.

"They just kind of fall into my lap," Catherine said. "I met Nicholas at a gallery in Northeast Harbor a few weeks back, and well... we just hit it off."

"Maybe you need to develop your interest in art," I suggested to Charlene.

"It might be worth considering," Charlene mused. "So," she asked Catherine, "does this mean Murray Selfridge is back on the market?"

"Does this mean you're interested?" I asked.

"I don't think he's my type, but I'm just wondering."

Catherine pursed her lips. "We've been having some differences of opinion," she said primly.

"Does that difference of opinion have anything to do with the new pier he's thinking about putting in?"

"Among other things," she said.

"So what's the skinny?" Charlene asked, pushing a strand of caramel-colored hair out of her eyes. "Did Francine talk him into another big development?"

"She bought two parcels of land by the lighthouse, and Murray owns the third. She needed him to make the whole thing work. She offered him good terms, and well..." She shrugged an elegant shoulder. "You know Murray."

"I hear Ingrid and Tom may be on board," Charlene said. "How did they manage that?"

"They made a nice offer for the lighthouse, and said a portion of the profits will go to the school," Catherine said. "Tom's really concerned about keeping the school viable—he's got kids there—and Ingrid, as you know, is big on island beautification."

"Don't they have to have an island-wide vote, though, to make it work?"

She shook her head. "Unfortunately, they don't. What they'll need to do, though, is figure out how to get people from the mainland here. So far, George hasn't been too amenable to the idea." George McLeod was the captain of the *Island Queen*, the mail boat that provided transportation to and from Cranberry Island. "Personally, I think it's a terrible idea, but I have to admit, it could be good for your business, Natalie," she said. "Although I'm sure they're planning on building accommodations near the lighthouse."

"A second pier would completely change the island," Charlene said.

"It would," Catherine said. "And not for the better." She sniffed. "Which is why I told Murray if he agreed to go along with it, I wouldn't date him anymore."

"You what?" I asked.

"You heard me," she said. "I'm standing on principle. Plus," she added, "there are a few other things I'm not crazy about."

There were a lot of things I wasn't crazy about when it came to Murray. I was curious what her list looked like.

"What did he say?" Charlene asked. "He's totally smitten with you!"

"He said I'll come around," she told me. "I said I would... but only if he didn't go along with this harebrained idea of his."

"Good for you!" I told her.

"I don't think he believed me," she said. "In fact, that's part of the problem. Lately, he's been a bit... callous, I guess. That's why I was okay with the date with Nicholas." She played with the pearls at her graceful throat, and her eyes took on a misty appearance. "But we did have a really magical time together..."

Nicholas certainly was better-looking than Murray, I thought. And his personality could hardly help but be better. "When are they deciding on the pier?" I asked, bringing Catherine back from whatever romantic yachting fantasy she'd embarked on.

"The vote is in a few days," she said. "Although I don't know what's going to happen now that Francine has... passed. They might have to delay the vote."

I sipped at my own Irish coffee. "Who has the say now? I wonder. Gus?"

"If they were married for forty years, I imagine so," Catherine said. "It may take some time to get everything through probate, though, depending on whose name is on the deed."

"Maybe we could get it designated a historical

site," I mused.

"The lighthouse?"

"It does have the underground railroad history," I pointed out. We'd discovered during the initial renovation a few years back that the lighthouse had been a waypoint for escaped slaves.

"It's worth thinking about," Charlene said, "but right now, I'm a little more worried about the fact that we seem to have another murderer on the island." She took another sip of her coffee. "Have you heard anything about Rainy?"

"Why would I hear anything about Rainy?" Catherine asked.

"Oh, that's right... you weren't here! She's one of the yoga folks. John and I found her unconscious out on the cliffs."

"Do you think the same person who... well, who did in that annoying woman went after one of the guests?"

"She was having some... er... personal problems," I said delicately.

"As in her boyfriend was making out with another woman," Charlene supplied, rather less delicately.

Catherine winced. "No wonder she was upset! How rude!"

Which was a little rich, I thought, considering she'd spent the night being wined and dined by Nicholas while Murray looked on jealously. I never imagined I'd feel bad for the developer, but there was a first time for everything.

"She did have a bump on her head, though," I said. "We don't really know if she fell and that knocked her out, or if it was the medication."

"What was she taking?"

"Klonopin. Quite a bit of it, actually, it seems."

"I've heard that stuff can be addictive. When did she disappear?"

"Last night," I said. "Why?"

"Someone else from the inn was out and about," she said. "I saw them come back at around two."

"What were you doing up at two?"

She turned a delicate shade of pink. "Texting."

"Uh-oh," Charlene said. "Murray's in trouble."

There was an awkward silence. Catherine examined her nails.

"Anyway, back to the person you saw out last night," I said, getting back to the topic at hand. "How do you know they were from the inn?"

"Whoever it was had a flashlight, and he or she came in the back door."

"So you couldn't tell if it was a man or a woman?"

"No," she said. "Are you thinking maybe whoever it was did in Rainy?"

"She left the inn last night, and as far as we know, she didn't come back."

"But we don't know that," Charlene pointed out. "Maybe she went out really early this morning."

"But Ravi said she didn't sleep in the room last night," I said. "Maybe she didn't. Maybe she slept on the couch downstairs. Or maybe he's lying."

I sighed. "Even if someone from the inn attacked Rainy, it doesn't explain what happened to Francine."

"You think they're connected?" Charlene asked.

"They both suffered bumps on the head," I said. "One a little more extreme than the other, but still."

"But Rainy might have passed out because of the Klonopin," Charlene said.

"True. But I wonder. Willow's yoga studio is based out of Florida. Francine Hodges was from that area." I forked up a piece of chocolate cake and considered it. "It seems like a weird coincidence, don't you think?"

"It does, now that you mention it," Catherine said. "Cranberry Island isn't exactly a well-known resort town. I mean, the inn is lovely, as is the island, but I'd expect a yoga retreat to be somewhere like Hawaii, or California, or something."

"Maybe I should move there," Charlene grumbled.

Catherine blinked. "Move?" "She's talking about getting a job in Portland," I told Catherine. "Please help me talk her out of it."

"What?" Charlene said. "It's simple numbers. There are bound to be a lot more men in an urban area."

"What about Alex?"

Charlene let out a heavy sigh. "He's totally unreliable," she said. "Besides, he's never going to want to settle down here. And even if he did, do I really want to be with someone who's hardly ever around?"

"As a woman who spent a significant portion of her life married, I'll say that does have its benefits," Catherine said with a crooked smile. "I think Natalie's right, though. You don't need to go to Portland to find a man. Maybe you should spend a little more time on Mount Desert Island."

"I guess," Charlene said, sounding unconvinced. "Is there more cake?"

"There is," I said, and cut her another slice. My heart hurt for my friend, and although I wasn't sure Alex was the right man for her, I was still irritated at him.

It was after nine by the time Charlene headed home. Willow was tidying up the yoga mats when I went out to the parlor a few minutes later. Her eyes were red, as if she'd been crying.

"How's it going?" I asked.

"Terrible," she said. "Rainy's in the hospital, and James is acting like he's never met me before, and..." She took a deep, shuddery breath. "I'm sorry. You don't need to hear this."

"I'm happy to listen," I said, putting a hand on her sculpted shoulder. "Do you want to come to the kitchen and have a cup of tea?"

"I'd love that, to be honest," she said. "Sequoia went up to bed early, and I have to be on for the retreat participants, and I have no one to talk to."

"Leave the yoga mats for later," I suggested, and led her to the kitchen, where I put the kettle on. "Would you like a piece of cake?" I asked. "I think Charlene left a little bit."

"That sounds great," she said, and I cut two slim slices of cake as she sat down at my big pine table. It wouldn't do to let her eat alone, after all.

"It's got to be hard running the retreat with your ex-boyfriend in it," I said as I slid a plate of cake across the table to her and sat down across from her with my own plate.

"It's a nightmare," she said. "I'm not really surprised he's here, though. He seems able to just kind of box things up and not think about them. Unless he's obsessed with something, that is."

"Like food?"

"Oh, totally," she said, cutting a piece of cake. "If I ate this while we were together, I wouldn't hear the end of it for a week."

"Sounds kind of controlling," I said.

"He is," she said. "He had a fiancée who died a while back; I've always wondered if that had something to do with it."

"How tragic," I said. "What happened?"

"He refuses to talk about it," Willow said. "Or refused anyway. We don't really talk at all now. I might as well be another piece of furniture." She stabbed at a piece of cake. "I know I shouldn't think this way, but it makes me wonder if he ever had feelings for me at all."

"I'm sure he did," I said. "If you don't mind my asking, why did you break up?"

She gave me a haunted look. "I don't know. He just said... we weren't right for each other." She squeezed her eyes shut, and a tear rolled down her cheek. "I'm sorry. It wasn't that it was perfect, it was just... I loved him. Or I thought I did."

"I know how that is," I said softly. I'd been dumped myself.

"The thing is, I wouldn't even be having this retreat on Cranberry Island if it wasn't for him. It was his idea. And now I have to see him all day, every day, and still be perky."

My antennae perked up. "It was his idea to hold the retreat, or to hold the retreat on Cranberry Island?"

"On the island, I mean. He said he'd heard Maine

was beautiful in the summer. And Florida is just so darned hot..."

"I lived in Texas," I said. "I remember. What made him pick Cranberry Island, though, do you know? It's kind of off the beaten path."

"He never said. Maybe he saw an article about it or something. I'd ask him, but he's not really talking to me."

"I get it," I said. The kettle whistled, and I stood up to fix a pot of tea. "Decaf?"

"Please," she said. "Otherwise I'll be up all night."

I plopped a couple of tea bags into a teapot and filled it with boiling water, then carried it to the table, along with two cups. As it steeped, I took a pot of milk from the fridge and carried it to the table, along with the sugar bowl.

"Enough about me, though," Willow said when I sat back down. "Rainy's in the hospital, and here I am complaining about a relationship that didn't work out."

"It's still valid to be upset," I said. "It's not about comparing situations."

"I guess you're right." She speared another piece of cake and chewed it mechanically.

"How long had Rainy been a part of the yoga studio staff?" I asked.

"Only a couple of months," she said. "She was... is... a quick learner, though. She just finished her certification last summer."

"Have she and Ravi been together the whole time?"

She nodded. "I think they met in some kind of support group or something. About a year ago, I think she told me."

I poured two cups of tea and slid one across the table to her. "They don't seem like a particularly happy couple."

"They argue a lot, and he makes a lot of bad choices. I think she could do better, but what do I know? I dated a robot who dumped me." She dashed some milk into her tea—no sugar—and took a long swig.

"Do you think he might be responsible for what happened to her?"

"I don't know," she said, putting down the cup. "I don't think so, somehow. He just seemed too... weak to do something like that. He's more reactive than proactive; I think he's too passive to actually try to hurt Rainy."

"I know what you mean," I said, although privately I wondered. I couldn't see him whacking anyone with a brick, but somehow, I wouldn't put it past him to slip her a few extra Klonopin. Had he given her some so he could sneak off to be with Kellie? Was that where he'd been after leaving my sofa?

"What kind of support group, do you know?" I asked.

She shook her head. "She kind of kept that quiet. With the Klonopin, though, I'm wondering if it might not be something related to addiction. And if they met there... of course it makes sense he might be unstable."

I'd mention that to John when I saw him next, I decided. But now, I was focused on Willow. "Look," I told her, "you're beautiful. You're charismatic. You're accomplished. There have got to be scores of guys out there who'd love to be with you."

"I just can't seem to find them," Willow said.

"You and Charlene both," I said. "She's thinking of moving to a city to up her odds of meeting Mr. Right. Or even Mr. Right Now."

"She's leaving the island?"

"Talking about it anyway," I said. "She's dating a naturalist who came to town to visit, but he seems more interested in spending time with the local fauna than with her."

"Men," Willow said sourly. She scraped more frosting off her plate.

Although I was very happy with the man I'd settled down with, I understood her feelings; I'd shared them in the past.

"I should probably head to bed," she said, pushing away the cake plate.

"Tomorrow will look brighter," I said.

"I hope so," she replied. "Thanks for the tea and cake; I'm feeling better."

"I'm glad."

She sighed. "Let's just hope someone else doesn't end up half-dead—or worse—before breakfast."

CHAPTER TWELVE

I WAS MIXING BATTER FOR A coffee cake when John came into the kitchen looking for me. It had been almost an hour since Willow had headed upstairs, and I was busy trying to figure out what the connection might be between Rainy and Francine... if there was one. Both had ended up outside with head injuries, but Francine's hadn't involved drugs—at least not that I knew of—and it was unclear whether someone had hit Rainy or if she'd knocked her head against a rock when she fell.

"What's going on in here?" John asked as I measured out flour.

"I'm making a cake for breakfast and trying to figure out what's going on on the island, that's all," I said.

"Cake? You're brave."

"Desperate times call for desperate measures," I replied as he eyed the batter bowl with interest. "You can lick the beaters when I'm done," I told him with a smile.

"We'll share," he offered. "One each."

"It's a deal," I said as I folded the flour into the batter. "Any news on Rainy or Francine?"

"Rainy's stable but still unconscious, last I heard," he said. "No autopsy results back on Francine yet, but Claudette is definitely the top suspect."

"I know it's not her," I said as I mixed in berries and then turned the batter into a pan.

"Who else do you have in mind?"

"It could be anyone in the co-op, for starters," I said. "She was killed with a brick from one of the traps, after all, and she was found right next to the co-op."

"What was she doing down there anyway, do you think?" he asked.

"Good question. Her husband didn't seem to even know she'd gone out."

"The co-op's not on the way back to her house from the inn," he said.

"No, it's not," I agreed. "Do you think she was meeting someone?"

"Or trying to attack the goats?"

"That's a possibility," I said. "I don't like it, but one of the goats was hurt, and she was carrying a knife."

"And she had threatened them," John added.

"It could be an angry lobsterman, though," I said.

"Who? Tom Lockhart?"

"Maybe. And there's also the board of selectmen. I heard she and Ingrid got into it, too; Francine was going to run for her spot, I think."

"No one would have voted for her, though. Plus, the elections aren't until next year. Not much of a motive."

I sighed. "Do you think maybe her husband got fed up with her?"

"After forty years, what could possibly have

changed?"

"Maybe being stuck on an island with her," I suggested. "Weren't they in a city in Florida?"

"Somewhere on the east coast, yes," he said. "I suppose there were a few more options for escape. It's kind of odd to move somewhere so much colder, and more remote, at least relatively speaking."

"They kept the house in Florida, though."

"So they were planning on being summer people," John said.

"Yeah," I said. "It'll be interesting to see what Gus chooses to do now that Francine is gone."

"That doesn't help us with our murder problem, though."

"Or a potential connection between Francine and Rainy."

"Maybe Rainy knew something or saw something she shouldn't have," John suggested.

"The yoga studio is based in Florida," I said. "Do you think maybe someone at the retreat knew Francine beforehand?"

"It's possible," he said. "Not everyone's from Florida, though. Kellie and her posse are from Texas."

I slid the cake into the oven and sighed. "There's something here I'm missing. I just wish I knew what it was."

"You think the two things are related?"

"I could be wrong, but I do," I confessed.

"So do I," John said.

"And I'm afraid if we don't figure it out soon, it won't be good for Claudette."

"It's a valid concern," he said, and sighed. "I've got to head down to my workshop and catch up a bit; all this excitement has put me behind on some of the stock for Island Artists."

"Want some company in a bit?"

"I'd love it, but only if you're up for it."

"Let me finish up this cake and I'll come down," I told him. He gave me a quick kiss and a hug, then headed out to his workshop.

As the cake baked, filling the kitchen with a delicious buttery scent, I went out to the dining room to tidy up for breakfast. I had just pushed through the kitchen door when I heard voices from the parlor.

"Are you sure you don't want me to return the favor?" The first voice was low and seductive.

"No... no. I'm just fine." The second voice, male, was high and reedy.

"Come on. It'll help relax you."

"Really. I'm fine... please, you've caused me enough trouble already. Just leave me alone."

"You seemed to like it the other day," came the petulant voice. "Come on. Nobody has to know."

"I told you. No."

Privacy was one thing, but this sounded an awful lot like sexual harassment. I marched through the dining room to the parlor. I was less than shocked to discover Kellie, wearing a very brief sports bra and skintight leggings, standing about a millimeter from Ravi, whom she appeared to have backed up against a wall.

"Everything okay?" I asked innocently, as if I hadn't heard what had happened.

"Fine," Ravi said, looking like a hunted animal.

"Would you like a cup of chamomile tea?" I offered him. "I know it's been a tough couple of days for you."

"Yes, please," he said. "I'll see you tomorrow," he told Kellie, who was looking at me with a slightly curled lip. She didn't appear to be pleased that I'd interrupted her seduction plans. Or assault plans, as the case may be. If she was the reason Rainy had taken the extra Klonopin...

"Thank you for intervening," he said when the swinging door had closed behind us.

"No problem," I said. "She doesn't take no for an answer, does she?"

"She doesn't," he agreed. "I think she's the kind of person who's always gotten her way."

I filled the kettle with water as he sat down at the table. "Is that what happened when you were giving her a massage?"

"Not completely, to be honest," he said, shrugging. "She's pretty, and things with Rainy and me... I'm ashamed to say it, but I didn't fob her off."

"You certainly were fobbing her off tonight," I pointed out as I put the kettle on.

"And she wasn't having any of it," he said glumly. "I can't believe I made that mistake with her. If I'd just not agreed to that massage, maybe Rainy wouldn't have taken all those pills and she wouldn't be in the hospital right now."

"You really care for her, don't you?" I asked gently.

"I do," he said. "Things between us have never been easy, but I love her."

"How did you meet?" I asked as I pulled the box of chamomile tea from the cabinet and filled the teapot with hot water to warm it.

"We met at a support group, actually." He glanced up at me. "I'm a little embarrassed to tell you about it, but we both had some issues with addiction."

"It's fairly common," I said. "I'm glad you both got help."

"That's part of why Rainy was so in to yoga," he said. "It was helping her with the cravings." His face crumpled. "And now this happened, all because of me..."

"We don't know what happened yet," I said. It was likely she'd taken several pills because of her upset with Ravi, but that wasn't certain. "We don't have all the facts. Besides, you didn't make her do anything. Although I will say, your judgment could have been a lot better."

"It could," he said. "I don't know if I'll ever be able to forgive myself."

"That's the thing. You can't change what happened, but you can bear it in mind going forward."

"It doesn't help Rainy, though, does it?"

"No," I said. "She's in good hands, though. She's young and healthy; hopefully, she'll come out of it just fine."

"And if she doesn't?"

"Let's not go borrowing trouble, okay?" I asked as the kettle whistled. I poured the hot water out of the teapot, added two tea bags, and filled the pot with boiling water. "I don't have any homemade cookies, but would you like some packaged short-bread? I keep some on hand for emergencies."

"I'd love some," he said. "I understand the reasoning behind all the diet stuff, but sometimes you just need a good cookie."

"I hear you," I said, retrieving a package of short-bread from the pantry and setting several cookies out on a plate. As he nibbled a wedge, I poured us both some tea and settled down across from him at the table. "I have a question for you that may or may not be related to Rainy."

"What is it?" he asked.

"Do you know if anyone on the retreat knew Francine Hodges before they came to the island?"

He blinked. "Francine Hodges? The lady who got killed down by the pier?"

"That's the one," I said.

"Why would anyone know her? Nobody on the retreat is from here."

"She's not from here either," I said. "She and her husband moved up from Florida a few months ago."

"That's a big transition," he said. "I'll bet they regret it come January. But no. I mean, someone would have told someone, right?"

"You'd think so," I agreed.

"I mean, the day she came into the inn talking about pressing charges about something? If anyone had known her, don't you think they would have said something?"

I cast my mind back to the night Francine died. Had anyone reacted strangely when Francine walked into the inn? And had Francine seemed to respond to anyone? Try as I might, I couldn't remember anything out of the ordinary. Then again, I hadn't been looking, and I'd been worried about Claudette.

"Did anyone talk about what happened that you know of?"

"Kellie thought she needed to settle down with a few martinis, and some of the other retreat participants thought it was funny when they found out why she was pressing charges. I mean, soy milk? That's not exactly a deadly weapon, you know? But no, other than that, no. And no one said anything about recognizing her. She was just kind of a crazy lady."

"How many of the retreat members knew each other beforehand?" I asked.

"Well, Sebastian and Gage are regulars, and of course there's Willow and Sequoia." Ravi ticked the names off on slender fingers. "James is from Florida, too, but the rest of them are from elsewhere."

"How did people outside of Florida find out about the retreat?"

"Willow did a webinar not long ago, and a few folks who did that decided to sign up." He took another bite of cookie and sipped some tea. "Do you really think someone at the retreat had something to do with what happened to Francine?"

"What does your gut say?" I asked. Of course, Ravi could be the killer, but he'd been so passive with Kellie, something told me he didn't have it in him to bean someone over the head with a brick.

"I think there's some tension going on between some of the retreat members, to be honest, but I can't think of anyone who would want to kill Francine."

"What kind of tension?"

"Well, Sebastian and Gage have been arguing a bit," he said. "And that woman Blue doesn't seem too happy with Kellie and her clone." He took another sip of tea. "I heard Blue scolding Kellie for making trouble yesterday."

"I get the feeling trouble is Kellie's specialty," I said. "What about Barbara Sue?"

"She just kind of falls in line with Kellie, from what I can see. She's been making eyes at James, though... both of them have. I think Barbara Sue actually likes him; Kellie just wants to conquer every man she meets."

"I've known people like that," I told him. "Male and female."

"I can't believe I fell for it."

I turned my cup around. "Do you really love Rainy?"

"I do," he said. "I wasn't sure, but now that she's hurt... it makes me realize how much she means to me."

"Maybe you should tell her," I suggested.

"She'd better recover," he said, and tears filled his eyes. "Do you know what the prognosis is?"

"Why don't you go visit her?" I said. "Maybe hearing your voice will help her come to, somehow.

"Maybe," he said glumly. "Or maybe I'll make things worse."

I looked at him with pity. I wasn't sure which way it would go either.

CHAPTER THIRTEEN

CHARLENE WAS STUDYING THE CLAS-SIFIEDS in the Portland newspaper when I pulled up a stool at the counter the next morning. Gwen had taken care of breakfast that morning, giving me a chance to head over to the store.

"You're here early," she said.

"I needed a break from the yoga crowd," I told her. My friend hadn't done her makeup, and her caramel-streaked hair was pulled back in a scrunchy; the dark circles under her eyes told me she hadn't slept well. "What's up with Alex?"

"He's barely here, as usual," she said. "I thought he was coming to visit me, but evidently the lobstermen are more intriguing."

"Still thinking of leaving town?" I asked.

"Considering it," she said. "None of the jobs are blowing me away, though. I don't want to be a deli clerk, and I don't think I'd make a particularly good dental hygienist."

"Plus, I doubt that's a train-on-the-job kind of thing."

She sighed and looked up from the page of job listings. "I'm so disappointed with Alex. I really thought we had something good together. Another pipe dream, I guess." She looked away and touched her eyes with the tips of her fingers, wiping away a bit of extra moisture, then straightened up. "I'm not going to mope, though; I'm a woman of action. If I don't want to be single for the rest of my life, I'm going to have to take things into my own hands."

"I agree with you," I said, "but moving to Portland seems like a bit of a big step. Are you still against dating locally? Bangor isn't that far away, and it's more of a metropolis."

"How am I going to meet anyone in Bangor if I'm here on Cranberry Island?"

"Maybe it's time to join the twenty-first century and get online," I said. "I'll take pictures, help you write the profile... whatever you need."

"I guess," she said noncommittally. "I've heard some horror stories about people ghosting you."

"That can happen no matter how you meet someone," I pointed out.

She pulled her mouth to the side; I knew we were both thinking of Alex. "True," she admitted.

"And in the meantime," I added, "you can help me figure out who hit Francine over the head with a brick so Claudette doesn't end up spending her golden years behind bars."

"They're still thinking she did it?"

"They haven't come up with any good alternatives," I said. John had told me that morning that the detectives were coming back to the island to ask Claudette and Eli more questions... and possibly take her into custody.

"I know she wasn't responsible for what happened to Francine," Charlene said.

"Me too. But I don't know who is."

As I spoke, the front-door bells jingled, and Ingrid Sorenson walked in.

I hadn't seen her in a few weeks; although she looked fit and tanned, with more makeup than I was used to seeing and a pair of sparkly earrings that brought out the color in her light eyes, the firm set of her mouth told me she was troubled.

"Oh," she said, spotting us. "I was hoping I'd run into you."

"Me?" I asked. "Why?"

"I wanted to talk to you about the whole thing with Francine. I know everyone's thinking Claudette did it, but I'm sure she didn't."

"Why is that?"

"I've known Claudette for years. She was furious with Francine, but there's no way she would have hurt her. Besides," she said, "I heard the goats were nearby, and wounded."

"That's right," I said. "Claudette never would have left Muffin and Pudge with untended wounds. And why leave the goats there, near the scene of the crime?"

"Exactly," Ingrid said. "Who would leave something that was so obviously a clue? Unless you were trying to frame someone else, that is."

"So it was probably an islander, unfortunately," Charlene said. "No one else would have known about the goat feud."

"Wait a moment," I said. "That's not true. When Francine came to the inn to say she wanted to press charges, everyone there heard her talk about the goats."

"But why would anyone at the retreat want to do in Francine?" Charlene asked. "I mean, she was pretty much a boil on the island, but they could all go home without worrying about their neighborhoods being destroyed." She tapped the paper thoughtfully. "Speaking of neighborhoods, I hear Murray and Francine had some kind of scheme cooked up."

"They did," I said. "That's part of why Murray and Catherine are on the outs."

"I heard she was out with one of the summer people from Northeast Harbor," Ingrid said. "Did she and Murray break up, then?"

"No," I replied. "At least not that I know of."

"Dating has got to be a challenge on an island as small as this," Ingrid commented.

Charlene rolled her eyes. "No kidding. Why do you think I'm looking at the Portland want ads?"

Ingrid blinked at her. "You can't be thinking of leaving! What would we do without you?"

"I'm sure you'd find someone to take over," Charlene said, although there was a sad look on her face as her eyes swept the cozy little store. The front, which was filled with squashy sofas and a beaten-up coffee table I was sure Francine had hated, was the island's "living room," where locals washed up regularly to share a cup of tea or coffee and the latest gossip. And, if I was on top of things, a few treats from the Gray Whale Inn, which I had been remiss in providing this week.

"So, the reason you're considering leaving is that you don't have a man. Is that right?"

Charlene shifted on her stool. "It sounds really bad when you put it like that."

Ingrid leaned forward. "I've been married for almost forty years." She glanced over her shoulder before continuing in a lower voice. "Trust me. It's not exactly Cinderella and Prince Charming living happily ever after. I mean, sure, I love my husband, but..." She trailed off and took a big breath. "All I'm saying is, some days a cottage of my own on the other side of the island—or maybe another island altogether—sounds like it might not be such a bad deal." She straightened up. "Still, though, I understand the desire."

"So I should just give up on finding a partner altogether?" Charlene asked, crossing her arms.

"No," she said. "Of course not! It's just... be careful what you give up. That's all."

Charlene looked unconvinced. In fact, she looked angry. I couldn't entirely blame her.

"Oh," Ingrid said, her eyebrows rising.

"What?" Charlene asked a little sourly. "Have the name of a local convent you'd like to suggest?"

Before Ingrid could answer, the bell jingled again, and Eli walked in, his normally jaunty stride slow. He looked like he'd aged ten years in the last week.

I left Charlene and Ingrid and hurried over to greet him. "Are you okay?" I asked as he sank into the nearest couch.

"Haven't slept a wink," he volunteered. "Claudette's in a tizzy, police are comin' round to ask more questions, and I haven't the faintest idea who decided Francine Hodges would look better with a brick in her head."

As he spoke, the bells tinkled again, and Marge O'Leary walked in. Marge had helped me out at the inn a few years back, before Catherine had come to stay and before I'd married John. She'd transitioned to working for several summer people and year-rounders who needed and could afford household help.

She'd trimmed down since her violent ex went to jail; I'd heard the divorce had come through a year or two ago. Now, her graying hair was pulled back in a ponytail from her ruddy face, and there was a spring in her step that hadn't been there when we met.

"How you holdin' up?" she asked Eli when she spotted him on the couch.

"Not too well, if I'm honest," he replied. "I'm supposed to be working on Gary's boat, but I just don't have the heart for it today."

"It'll come," I said soothingly.

"He needs the boat for work," Eli said. "I'm going to have to get after it this afternoon for sure."

"I knew those Hodges were trouble as soon as they set foot on the island," Marge said. "That woman thought she was royalty, her poor husband runnin' around behind her, tryin' to clean up her messes."

"You work for the Hodges, don't you?" I remembered someone mentioning she'd taken the job after Francine had fired two other housekeepers.

"I must be a masochist, but yes. At least the money's good. And with Francine off the premises, things are a whole lot easier."

"Can I buy you both a cup of coffee?" I asked.

Marge glanced at her watch. "I've got a few minutes," she said. "You could twist my arm."

"Sit right here," I said. "Cream and sugar?"

"Both," they both said.

"But not a word to Claudette!" Eli added as I walked up to the counter.

"Go ahead," Charlene said, and I poured coffee for them and returned to the couches; Charlene knew I'd settle up later.

"What did you think of the Hodges?" I asked as I handed Marge a cup of coffee.

"She was a piece of work," Marge said.

"I heard someone vandalized the house not long before she died," I said. "Did she have any theories as to who that might be?"

"The list was long, I can tell you that," she said, taking a sip of her coffee and glancing at Eli. "Your sweet wife, of course, although I know she wouldn't hurt a fly."

"Tell the detectives that," Eli said glumly.

"I will if they ask," she promised.

"Who else?" I asked.

"Half the lobster co-op," she said. "The lobster pound, Berta Simmons, and the rest of the merchants on the pier were none too pleased with her harebrained idea to put a pier on the rockiest part of the island." Berta sold sea glass mobiles and jewelry and had been scouring the island for materials for years. "But here's the thing..." She leaned forward. "Just two days before she met her maker, she got another card. She said to her husband it was just like in Florida."

"What did she mean by that?"

"I don't know," she said, "but her hubby, he said, 'That's why we left. We left all that behind.'" She glanced around. "And then he said, 'You'd better be careful you don't create the same situation here.' Well, she didn't like that, whatever that meant. Didn't talk to him for more than a day, from what I could see."

"What did she leave behind?" I asked.

"That's the question, isn't it?" Marge said. "It sounds like she wasn't too popular back at home, either. Maybe that's why she moved to an island as far away as possible."

"Sounds like she's no stranger to threats," I said.

"Small wonder," Ingrid said, walking up behind us. "She was a human bulldozer. If she didn't like your ideas, she'd do everything she could to roll right over you."

"That's right; she was going to run against you on the board of selectmen, wasn't she?" I asked.

"She'd never have won, but that was what she was planning to do, yes. And she managed to trump Catherine and get Murray to go along with her new idea. She bought that land out by the lighthouse for next to nothing."

"Who sold it to her?" I asked.

"There was an off-island family who bought the point from a lobstering family several years ago, planning to build. They ended up in Somesville instead; they didn't like having to take the mail boat, evidently. She tracked them down and offered them cash, and they took it." Ingrid grimaced. "And then she had her eye on the lighthouse, too."

"Doesn't the town own that?"

"They don't own the lighthouse, no, but with Francine on the board of selectmen and some cash for the renovation and the lobster co-op, I'm guessing she thought she could strong-arm her plans through. Murray owned the land next to the point; they were working on a deal together."

"But wasn't the lighthouse put there because of the dangerous rocks?" I asked. "Hardly the place for a pier."

"They were going to dredge it, and build it up into a harbor of sorts," Ingrid said. "I'm not sure what the plan was. Or if it's dead in the water, so to speak, with Francine's passing." She grimaced.

"I certainly hope it is," I said. "So we've got lots of extra suspects now. The merchants, the co-op... although if Francine was going to give them money, would they have wanted her out of the way?"

"She was planning on changing the way this island has run for centuries. And remember, she was planning on moving the co-op to the other side of the island... and she was constantly complaining about the smell of bait and trap storage. I think she thought she could buy everyone out."

"She was wrong," I said. "The question is, who decided on a permanent solution?" I turned to Marge. "I hate to ask this, but do you think her husband might have gotten tired of her after forty years?"

Ingrid shuffled from foot to foot, looking uncomfortable as she took a sip of coffee.

"My gut says no, but you never can tell, can you?" Marge offered. "I put up with a lot, the Lord knows," she added, referencing her murderous husband. "But I'm not sure I could put up with forty years of Francine Hodges."

"One more question," I said. "She came to the inn the night she died. Did you see her at all after that?"

Marge shook her head. "I came to work the next day, but Mr. Hodges told me to go home."

"What time was that?"

"Nine o'clock," she told me.

"Did he often do that?" I asked.

She shook her head. "Not that I can recall. She called all the shots around the place."

"Did he say why, or look upset?"

"He looked... rattled, I guess you could say. He said someone had spray-painted the house the night before. He didn't want to disturb any evidence before the police could look at it. He didn't say a thing about his wife not coming home, though."

"He told me it had been spray-painted, too," I said. "And he showed me the threats. But he didn't seem to take them seriously... even though his wife had been killed."

"That does seem odd," Charlene said. She had joined me on the couch while we were talking. "But grief does funny things."

"Do you think he *is* grieving?" I asked.

"You don't live with someone for forty years and not grieve, I think," Ingrid said. "You share a life— even if it's a twisted life. When the other half isn't there anymore, I imagine it's a shock."

Marge nodded. "When Eddie went to jail, at first I was relieved. Excited, almost. But there was a time there when it felt empty. I didn't know who I was when I wasn't married to Eddie, awful as he was."

"You make marriage sound amazing," Charlene said, rolling her eyes.

"I think it all depends on the marriage," Ingrid said. "But the most important thing here is finding out what really happened to Francine Hodges, before someone we care about gets blamed for the crime."

Charlene sighed. "It's a shame really. In some

ways, whoever did it performed a public service."

"Truth will out," Marge said in a stertorous voice that made us all look up in surprise.

What was the truth? I wondered. There was more here than met the eye, that much I knew.

But how was I going to find out what it was?

CHAPTER FOURTEEN

ON THE WAY HOME, I decided to take a detour and swing by the co-op. I knocked before walking into the small space, which always felt like a living history museum to me in some ways, despite the computer setup at one end of it, where Tom Lockhart managed the co-op's business. Although it was lined with small windows, the building still felt dark inside, with unfinished, smoke-stained board walls and a weathered wooden floor. The woodstove in the corner was cold because it was summer, and the whole place smelled like a slightly revolting yet comforting blend of kerosene, herring, spilled beer, burned coffee, and less-than-fresh laundry.

The place was fairly quiet because almost everyone was out on their boats. Adam and Tom were staring at a screen full of figures on the computer. The only other person in the co-op was a heavyset lobsterman in bright yellow rubber boots, who was sitting in a dark corner moodily sipping a cup of very murky-looking coffee.

"Hi, Natalie. What's up?" Adam asked, turning from the computer. "Need a few more lobsters?"

"Not today, thanks," I said. "Just thought I'd stop

by to say hi."

"And nose around into what happened to that Francine woman," added the lobsterman from the corner.

"Well, maybe some of that, too," I confessed, trying not to blush. "Do you have any ideas?"

"Could be anyone," said the lobsterman. It was Gary; he'd been there when Francine was found. It must be his boat Eli was working on... or not working on, as the case might be. "Nobody wanted her here."

"She was kind of a bull in a china shop."

"Summer people," the man scoffed.

"I heard she was more of a year-round person," I said.

"Cancer on the island," he said shortly. "What islander has a problem with traps stacked outside? It's a working island, not some hoity-toity resort."

"So she went after you, did she?"

"Ayuh," he replied with a sharp nod. "Left notes on the traps. Scolded me in the street. We was here for hundreds of years before she and her kind ever set foot on this island. Now, just because she can afford a fancy house, she thinks the rest of us ought to change how we've been living."

"Well, she doesn't think that anymore," I pointed out. "Sounds like she made a lot of folks mad."

"That's the truth," he said.

"Anyone angry enough to hit her over the head with a brick?" I asked bluntly.

He looked away and shrugged, then took a swig of coffee. "I don't know nothin' about what happened to her."

Which I sensed wasn't entirely true. I could feel

that the conversation had caught Tom and Adam's attention, too; they had grown still and quiet.

I sat down on one of the rickety chairs a few yards from Gary. "What do you think she was doing down here at the co-op?"

"Probably tryin' to burn the place down," he suggested. "I heard she had a lighter on her. And a knife for goin' after Claudette's poor goats."

So much for crime scene secrets, I thought. "Wouldn't you think you'd want more than a lighter if you were trying to burn a place down?"

Gary looked around. "This place is half-soaked in kerosene and fish oil. I don't think you'd need much to send it up in smoke."

"But why would you want to?" I asked. "I mean, wasn't she planning on building a new pier out by the lighthouse? I thought the point was to leave this one for the lobstermen. No point in burning it down."

"Actually, Gary has a point. She thought it was ugly," Tom added. "She wanted us to rebuild it."

"You really think she came down here to do arson?" I asked.

Tom shrugged. "I think she'd do just about anything to impose her vision on Cranberry Island."

"Was anyone down here the night she died?" I asked.

"I was, actually," Tom said.

"What? When?"

"I was down here until around one," he said. "I installed some new software the other day, and I was trying to get it to work."

"Did you hear or see anything?"

"I did, now that you mention it," he said. "Muffin and Pudge were nearby, as you know, in the field just up from the dock. They started bleating at around midnight. After a few minutes, I went to check on them, but I didn't see anything wrong. I didn't look too closely, though... it was dark." He grimaced. "If that's when someone attacked them, there's a good chance they were gone by the time I stepped outside; I didn't go out for a few minutes."

"So when you left the co-op, you went out this door, right?"

"It's the only door," he pointed out.

"And Francine was on the other side of the co-op. So if she was already there, you wouldn't have seen her."

"True," he said.

"She couldn't have been there at midnight," Adam said. "High tide was at eleven that night. From what I saw, her body wasn't far below the high-tide line. If it had been earlier, she would likely have been washed out to sea."

"Which leads to an interesting question: Why leave her there for everyone to find? Why not just push the body out to sea?"

Adam's eyebrows rose. "Whoever it was must have wanted her to be discovered."

"But why?" I asked.

"Because there was something about her that would incriminate someone other than the murderer," Adam said.

"That's what I think, too." I turned to Gary. "Are you sure you don't know anything about what happened to Francine that night?"

"Well," he said, his eyes shifting, "I might have seen something."

"What?"

He looked a bit pink. "There's been a few folks from the mainland moving into our territory," he said. "I was out patrolling, looking to see if any of their traps might have migrated to the wrong place. I saw a light bobbing not too far from the co-op."

"I wondered whose boat that was," Tom said, fixing him with a keen look. "That was around the time I heard the goats. Are you sure you were just... patrolling?"

"Of course," Gary said, meeting his eyes with a steady gaze. "Just lookin', that's all." We all knew that "looking" worked better in daylight; I was guessing he was cutting an interloper's gear, but I wasn't going to say anything. The last thing I needed to do was get involved in the lobstermen's version of a turf war. If there was something to be dealt with, I knew Tom would take care of it.

"Where was the light coming from?" I asked, pulling Gary back to the subject at hand.

"Down the hill," he said. "From your end of the island, actually."

One of my guests? I wondered. There were a few houses on my end, but the bulk of the population lived on the other side of the island.

"It stopped off by the goats," he continued, "and then bounced back a ways up the hill before it disappeared."

"Disappeared? Like, into the trees or behind a building?"

"Naw," he said, shaking his head. "I think whoever it was just flipped the light off. It looked to me like whoever it was was in the middle of the field."

"Why would you turn your light off in the middle of the field?" Tom asked.

"You'd do it if you were waiting for someone," I suggested. "And if you didn't want them to see you."

"Are you thinking someone arranged to meet Francine by the co-op?" Adam asked.

"It's a theory," I said, and turned back to Gary. "You're sure you didn't see anyone else?"

"That's all I saw," he said. "Think I might have seen a murderer?"

"It's a possibility," I said, thinking it might be time to stop off to see Gus Hodges again. "Sure you didn't see anything else?"

"I'm sure," he said, and Tom echoed him.

"Well, if you think of anything else, please let someone know. Claudette is going to need all the help she can get."

❧ ❧

My next stop was the Hodges' house. I took the long way from the co-op, although I confess the beautiful day was somewhat wasted on me. Although the blueberry bushes were festooned in pale little bell-shaped flowers and the green, verdant moss beneath the trees looked like fairy carpet, my thoughts kept returning to Francine Hodges.

Whoever killed her had either panicked and fled the scene or had left her there intentionally because they wanted her found. My instinct leaned toward the second explanation.

She'd definitely been found with some potentially incriminating evidence. First, there was the knife, which pointed to a run-in with Muffin and Pudge. Now that I thought about it, though, it didn't seem like the kind of knife someone like Francine Hodges would have. It was a utility knife, not a high-end kitchen knife. Where would she find something like that? And why would she be out and about on the island with a knife? It was possible she wanted to attack the goats, but was she carrying it for self-defense? Considering the notes she'd recently received, that idea had merit. But if you were under threat, why go wandering around the island in the middle of the night?

And second, the lighter. Again, why walk around with a lighter? A flashlight seemed like a better bet if you were trying to see where you were going. The night had been overcast, so there had been little moonlight to rely on. Was she really trying to burn down the co-op?

Or had whoever killed her planted both things to throw the cops off the scent?

As I ruminated over the evidence, the lighthouse came into view. The tall white spire had been erected long ago to warn sailors off the point... and the sharp rocks buried under the water's choppy surface. Not exactly a natural location for a harbor, although I knew the plan was to put the main pier a bit away from the lighthouse to avoid the worst of the rocks. It was a pretty piece of property, with a lovely view of Sutton Island, which sheltered it somewhat from the Gulf of Maine, and a long, green tongue of Mount Desert Island in the distance. A few eider ducks bobbed on the waves, and the green swath of the meadow was studded with pink and purple lupines, most of which I was sure would be decimated if Murray and Francine's plans were put into place. Although the lighthouse looked like an ivory pillar from a distance, I knew that up close the paint was peeling, and the windows had been boarded up for some time.

The plans to renovate the place had never quite come to fruition; some said it was because of the ghost who resided there, but I personally thought it was because most islanders really didn't want another tourist attraction drawing summer people. Although it would be good for my business, I respected the islanders' desire to keep some of their culture intact. Oddly, even those who didn't care much for summer people were glad they had a place to direct lost outsiders to. Before I started the inn, from time to time day trippers would miss the last boat and go from door-to-door, knocking to ask for a place to stay. These days, I got a few such guests every summer; I think the rest of the locals were happy to have someone to take wayward visitors off their hands.

As I stared at the lonely lighthouse, perched on craggy granite and surrounded by wild but beautiful land, I knew Francine and Murray's vision had no place here. I turned away, heading down the road toward the Hodges' house, wondering if someone else with the same ideas had decided to take things into his or her own hands.

And if Murray Selfridge might not want to watch his back.

Catherine was only halfway through cleaning rooms when I got back to the inn a little after noon.

"How's it going?" I asked as she emerged from

one of the downstairs rooms looking a little mussed.

"Someone took some kind of oil bath in there," she said, wiping her forehead with the back of her hand. "It smells like an opium den, and it's hard to clean up."

"What does an opium den smell like?"

"I don't know, but I'm guessing it's something like that!" she replied, pointing back toward the bathroom. All I could smell was bleach, but I decided to trust her. "It's taken me almost an hour to get it cleared up; I'm running behind."

"Whose room is it, anyway?"

"Sequoia's," she said. "She's a big fan of patchouli, it seems."

"Why don't I do a few of the rooms?" I offered.

"Would you?" she asked. "That would be a big help. I'm supposed to go out with Murray tonight."

"Oh?"

"To talk," she said.

"Well, that sounds like progress."

"We'll see," she said darkly.

I decided not to pry, and we spent a few minutes divvying up the rooms. I headed back to the laundry room to grab some cleaning supplies and then tackled the first of the rooms.

First up was Kellie's; although her two cohorts were sharing a room, the queen of the threesome had claimed one of the biggest rooms at the inn.

Although Kellie always looked impeccably groomed, her room did not; it was a jumble of brightly colored yoga clothes, which were draped over every possible surface, high-end makeup, and a variety of scientific-sounding lotions and potions. I made the bed, trying not to disturb too much of the clothing, and did a quick clear-up of the bath-room, keeping my eye out for anything that might possibly be linked to Rainy... or to Francine.

I didn't run across anything interesting in Kellie's room, or in the adjacent one, which was occupied by Blue and Barbara Sue. Next was James's room, which, to my not-very-great surprise, looked prac-tically unoccupied... at least until you stepped into the bathroom. The bed was already made, with knife-edge corners, the dresser and night-table surfaces were clear of anything personal, and the only indication that someone had been there was a faint whiff of woodsy aftershave. With one excep-tion, I noticed as I walked through the room: There was one photo of James beside a beautiful young woman with dark, gleaming hair and a wide smile that reminded me a little of Julia Roberts. Who-ever she was, she certainly wasn't Willow. Had he been seeing the yoga instructor on false pretenses? Had he led her on? And if so, why... and why come to the retreat when you'd called it off with the retreat leader? Practicality was one thing, but com-mon decency suggested backing out would be the right thing to do. Knowing James, however, I was guessing practicality was the primary driver.

In contrast to the barren room, the bathroom counter was lined with bottles of supplements... There were at least fifteen in all, and I wondered how he managed to choke them down without throwing up. It was a fairly disappointing room all in all, at least from an investigatory standpoint, and I found myself curious about what I'd find in Willow's, which was—unfortunately for her—the next room down.

Like James's room, Willow's was neat, but unlike his, it wasn't completely spartan. The bed was made—which I was thankful for—but the night table held a water glass and two books on relationship troubles: *Getting Over Mr. Wrong* and *Finding True Love*. A spiral-bound notebook lay open on the desk by the window. Feeling mildly guilty, I glanced at the page. "I hate him. I hate him. I really do. I can't believe I let myself believe he was interested in me, when the whole time, he was only interested in her. Should I say something? I just don't know... it's ancient history. And I just can't believe he could be involved..."

The writing trailed off, and I blinked. She'd known he was interested in someone else. The woman in the picture on his night table? Someone else at the retreat? I tried to think of what I'd seen of James. If he was here to hit on someone else at the retreat, he'd been doing a very quiet job of it. Of the women from Florida, there was Sequoia, Virginia, and Rainy. Rainy. She'd been knocked out after her run-in with Ravi. Had James maybe come to try to convince Rainy to be with him instead? Had she refused, and he'd responded with violence?

It was a possibility; after all, someone had returned to the inn, according to Willow. If James was responsible for what happened to Rainy, that still didn't explain the brick embedded in Francine's head. Or was Willow jealous of Rainy? Had she decided to do her in herself?

Romance could be an absolute nightmare, I thought to myself as I dusted the desk and straightened the pair of sneakers she'd left next to the bathroom. I'd gotten lucky with John, and Gwen had found a good man in Adam. I just wished I could find a way for Charlene to connect with someone wonderful. I wasn't too worried about Catherine; she seemed to be able to hold her own, to say the least.

I finished tidying the room and stepped out into the hallway, almost knocking Willow over.

"Oh," she said. "I wasn't expecting to see you."

"Room tidying," I said, brandishing my bucket of cleaning supplies. "How are things going with the retreat?"

"As well as can be expected," she said. "At least the weather's cooperating; it's beautiful out there. We did hatha yoga right by the water; water's supposed to be very healing."

"I find it to be," I agreed.

"Any word on Rainy?"

I shook my head. "Nothing yet, but I haven't called recently, either."

"I should go do that," she said. "I'm worried about her."

I glanced down the hallway and dropped my voice. "How are you doing with James today?"

Her eyes darted to the desk behind me, widening when they spotted the open notebook. "I'm getting over it," she said. "Sometimes it's just not a good match, you know? The right guy will come along. Anyway, I'd better go freshen up; we've got an hour break before the next session, and I need to recharge. See you at dinner!"

She smiled and darted past me into the room, closing the door behind her and leaving me in deep thought. Willow wasn't over James, not by a long shot. The question was, who was James really interested in? And what did it have to do with what had happened to Rainy?

★★★

I'd just put away the cleaning supplies and pulled my recipe binder off the bookshelf when John walked into the kitchen, looking grim.

"What's wrong?" I asked.

"Rainy's still unconscious," he said. "And they took Claudette into custody."

I set down the binder. "What? Why?"

"The argument in the store. The lack of an alibi." He sat down and let out a long gust of air, as if he were deflating. "And the goats."

"I talked with Gary Hall at the co-op today," I said. "He was out...er, checking traps... and saw someone with a flashlight walk down to the meadow by the co-op in the middle of the night... before one, I think he said. Whoever it was came from our side of the island."

"That doesn't help matters," he replied. "Claudette lives on our side of the island. And the goats were in that meadow, which gave her a good reason to go down there." He cocked an eyebrow. "Checking traps at one in the morning? That wouldn't have anything to do with fishing territories, would it?"

"I know," I said. "Tom's got it, I presume. At any rate, we've got to find out what happened. I think it may be linked with the retreat, and if they all go home before we solve it..."

"We may never know what happened, and Claudette may spend the rest of her days in prison," John finished for me.

"Exactly," I said, staring at the binder. "I can't believe my friend's in jail and I'm worrying about dinner."

"You're not just worrying about dinner. If I know you, you've been out trying to solve this mystery all day, and now you're taking care of what needs to be done. Have you picked up the grocery order at the store yet?"

"Not yet. I don't think it had made it to the island when I was down there earlier."

"Why don't you go pick up the order and see if Charlene's picked up any gossip? In the meantime, I have to make a delivery to Island Artists. I'll ask around, see if anyone down there knows anything."

"That sounds like a good plan. And one more thing—" I said.

"What?"

I told him about the photo I'd seen in James's room... and the open journal in Willow's.

"You're sure it was open when you got to the room?"

"Yes," I said, rolling my eyes at him.

"You can't say you're not prone to snooping."

"I know, I know," I said. "But you have to admit, it's been helpful in the past."

He didn't respond.

"Anyway," I said, "I just looked at the page it was open to. I didn't touch anything."

"Who do you think she was talking about?" he asked.

"James, I imagine," I said. "The thing is, who was he so interested in? I haven't seen signs of interest in anything other than the calorie count of various menu items, honestly."

"I wonder what she meant by ancient history?"

"Was it someone he'd seen in the past, maybe?" I asked. "But the photo in his room doesn't resemble anyone at the retreat."

"Maybe you could talk to her."

"And what? Ask about what I saw in her journal?" I sighed. "She did open up to me about James a little bit the other day. I'm sure she's upset and would love someone to talk to; I know it must be hard being peppy all day when your ex is ten feet away."

"Catherine doesn't seem to be having that trouble," John commented.

"Are they broken up, then? I thought they were talking."

He sighed. "She's on the brink. I don't really like Murray that much, but I'm not sure two dates with Mr. Veuve Clicquot is a reason to call things off with someone you really seem to get along with."

"I thought she was just doing it to convince him to back off the development plans," I commented.

"I thought so, too, but apparently she kind of likes this guy."

I was about to respond when there was a tap on the door, and Willow walked into the kitchen, her face pale.

John exchanged glances with me and stood up. "I'm going to make that delivery to Island Artists," he said. "Do you want me to pick up the grocery order?"

"I'll give you a call," I said, and turned to Willow. "Come on in! Tea?"

"Sure," she said as John disappeared out the back door.

"Sit down," I said as I busied myself with the kettle. "You look upset; what's wrong?"

"Everything," she said glumly. "Everybody at the retreat is bickering, I don't know if Rainy's going to be okay, and James..." She burst into tears.

"That's been really hard for you, hasn't it?" I asked.

She nodded, and I handed her a tissue. She dabbed at her eyes and took a deep breath, struggling to get herself together.

"What happened with him, anyway?" I asked.

"I don't know," she said. Her eyes darted up to me, and then away. "He just lost interest, I guess."

"I've had that happen," I said. "Chamomile tea? Mint? Earl Grey?"

"Mint," she said, and I fished two mint tea bags out of the box, then swished out the teapot and filled it with hot water.

"What was his dating history like before you met?"

"Kind of sparse, I think," she said. "He's not the most flirtatious person on the planet. Good-looking, but not exactly a social butterfly."

"What about the fiancée you mentioned?" I asked, thinking of the photo in his room.

"He never talked much about her, though."

"You mentioned she died. Do you know how?"

"I don't know much about it really," she said. "He didn't talk about it much." She busied herself inspecting her short nails. "Anyway, that's ancient history."

Ancient history. The same words I'd seen in her journal. She was hiding something. But what?

CHAPTER FIFTEEN

I WAS ON MY WAY BACK from the store when I spotted a familiar figure down by the lobster co-op. It was Gus Hodges, standing not too far from where Francine had been found, staring out to sea.

I parked the van, thankful the cold food was safely stowed in coolers, and walked down to join him.

He jumped when I greeted him.

"Oh. I didn't hear you coming," he said.

"How's it going?" I asked.

"As well as can be expected, I suppose," he said after a moment's pause. "I loved Francine, but she was hard to live with. It's funny," he said. "For so many years I wondered what life would be like without her; I fantasized about it from time to time, to be honest. And now that she's gone..." He shrugged. "I just feel empty. Directionless." He made a small mark in the rocks with the toe of his leather loafer. "Lost, almost."

"It must be a huge change," I said.

"She was such a force," he said. "Unstoppable once she set her mind to something. It's hard to imagine someone was able to snuff it out, just like that." He snapped his fingers.

"It's tragic," I agreed. "It shouldn't have been that way."

"No," he mused. "No, it shouldn't. But I'm not completely surprised."

"You're not?"

"My wife spent the last four decades making people angry," he said. "I always told her it would catch up with her. I just didn't expect it to happen like this."

"Who else did she make angry?" I asked.

"Who *didn't* she make angry?" he replied. "It's a much shorter list. I wouldn't have guessed Claudette White would be the one to put an end to her, though. I guess those goats were like children to her."

"Honestly, I'm not sure Claudette was the one responsible," I told him.

"But they arrested her," he said. "Surely they wouldn't have done that without proof."

"Mistakes have been made in the past," I told him. "If you have any idea who else might have wished your wife ill, please tell me. I'm afraid an innocent woman may go to prison."

He sighed. "There was whoever was sending those notes, I suppose."

"And whoever spray-painted your house," I pointed out. "Did you talk to the police about that?"

"I did," he said. "They figured it was just teen-agers."

"Did you give them the postcards, too?"

"I told them about them, yes," he said.

"Did you give them to them?"

"I think Marge must have burned them with the trash," he said. "I couldn't find them."

Brilliant. Another clue gone. I gazed out across the buoy-studded water to where a lobsterman moved from lobster pot to lobster pot, like a bee visiting flowers. I squinted at the buoy at the front of the boat; it wasn't one I recognized. One of the interlopers' boats from the mainland? If so, they had a lot of nerve; they were within spitting distance of the co-op.

"I've been wondering," I said idly as the boat turned toward the mainland and puttered off into the distance. "Why did you and Francine decide to move to Maine?"

He gave me a sidelong look. "Well, we're really just summer people… and the official story is that we were looking for a change of pace," he said, "but the truth is, there were threats."

"Threats?"

He sighed. "Like I said, she cut a wide swathe. She fought a lot of battles, and won them, too. Lots of folks were bitter."

"Bitter enough for you to move?"

He nodded. "Someone sent death threats."

"Death threats? Like the ones you got here?"

"Similar," he said, and his eyes widened. "You don't think those might be connected, do you?"

"It's possible."

"And there was an arson attempt," he said. "They burned down half our garage. If we hadn't caught it in time…" He shuddered.

"Did the police ever find out who did it?"

He shook his head. "Nope."

"Surely you had an idea who it might have been,

though?"

"They never said why they did it.. And I know Francine's made a lot of people angry; it could have been anyone."

"How did she make people angry?"

"She had lots of people who were furious with her."

"So you moved to escape the death threats?"

"Ironic, isn't it?" he asked, staring out at the water.

"It kind of is," I said. "Have you considered the possibility that someone followed you from Florida?"

"Do you think?" he asked. "But what about the mail boat? Everyone would know if a stranger came to the island."

"Maybe," I said. "You know the yoga retreat at the inn is from Florida, right?"

He blinked. "It is?"

"The studio that put it on is based in Pompano Beach," I said.

"That's just down the road from Fort Lauderdale!" he said.

"Those postcards; were they anything like the threats you received in Florida?"

"I don't know," he said.

I stifled a sigh. After forty years of having his life run by someone else, was he really that incapable of making simple connections? It sure looked like it. "Well, were they delivered in the same way? On postcards? Handwritten or typed?"

"I... I think they were letters," he said. "In Sharpie."

"Are you sure you didn't keep any of them? Even the threatening ones?"

"I didn't do the filing," he replied, looking away from me. "Francine would have taken care of that."

"Is there any way you could look and see?" I asked.

"I guess I could do that," he said. "If I still have them."

"Because if the murderer is still at large," I said, to give him a bit of motivation, "he or she might not stop at Francine."

Gus's eyes widened. "You don't mean... they might kill me?"

I shrugged. "You never know," I said. "I'd lock the doors if I were you."

He shoved his hands in his pockets. "I'd better go find those letters."

"Need a ride?" I asked. "The van's over there."

He glanced around, as if the murderer might have materialized on the rocky beach in the past thirty seconds. "No," he said. "I need my exercise. Besides," he said, "Francine was the one everyone wanted dead. Not me." He glanced at his watch. "Speaking of exercise, I think I'm going to start heading back."

"Take care of yourself," I said. "And please look for those postcards again."

"I will," he said in a tone of voice that didn't inspire confidence.

As I walked back to the van, I glanced back over my shoulder. Gus was headed up the shore at a brisk pace... but not in the direction of his house.

My instincts told me there was more to Gus than he was telling me. I watched until he followed the path into a stand of trees... and then I stepped away from the van and headed back down to the beach.

The path was narrow, and not frequently used; it climbed past several huge granite boulders, then wound through a grassy knoll and into a thick tangle of mixed woods. I walked slowly, avoiding dead branches. Although I couldn't see Gus, I knew he must be ahead of me somewhere.

I walked about a hundred yards before I heard voices. I slowed down, scanning the greenery for signs of Gus. I took a few more steps forward, being careful not to step on anything; then I spotted him.

He was talking to a woman with blond hair, but I couldn't see her face; her back was turned to me.

"I told you, it had nothing to do with us."

"Are you sure?" she said.

"I swear it," he replied. "When are you going to be free?"

"I... I just don't know," the woman replied. She was wearing blue, and her light hair flashed in the sun though the trees. "It hasn't been that long. I'm just not sure it's the right thing to do. I shouldn't be seeing you at all."

"He doesn't meet your needs," Gus said in a wheedling tone. "You've been unfulfilled for so many years. There's a reason I moved to Cranberry Island... It was you."

"But..."

"Shh," he said. "Stop thinking so much. Just be. Let me take care of you."

There was silence, and what appeared through the thick branches to be kissing. I felt my eyebrows rise almost to my hairline. I would never have taken Gus for a ladies' man... and who was his target?

The woman's voice was soft. "I always feel so good when I'm with you."

"When we're together, it will be like this all the time," he cooed. "I'll shower you with presents... you haven't seen anything yet. We were meant to be together."

More silence. Presumably kissing. I strained to see who it might be.

"I can't stay," she said finally. "I have to go."

"Are you sure?"

"Yes," she said firmly.

I took that as my cue to double back before I was spotted. After a last try at identifying the mystery woman, I hurried back down the trail, anxious to get back to the van before Gus spotted me. I'd just closed the door behind me when he reappeared, walking more slowly this time, and with something of a smug smile on his face.

For all his "lost" talk, he looked very much like a man with a plan. I was burning with curiosity to find out who he was just with; whoever it was must have been seeing someone else. But I didn't know of that many blondes on the island. There was the librarian Matilda, Ingrid... and Catherine.

Was Catherine seeing Gus on the side? Had Murray found out? And if so, where did Nicholas come into the equation?

And then there was Ingrid Sorenson. Ingrid, local selectwoman, the queen of propriety, who'd had a long-standing marriage, was a stalwart of the island, and was very invested in a proper appearance. Her struggles with her son's addiction issues had softened that stance a bit, but she still had a strong sense of right and wrong... and an affair would definitely fall on the "wrong" side of the equation. Was she really making out with Gus Hodges in the woods by the dock? It was possible, but I didn't know.

Gus was a dark horse, though, that much was sure.

And now I knew how he'd survived forty years with Francine.

CHAPTER SIXTEEN

A S I DROVE BACK TO the inn, I thought about
Gus, wondering if, in fact, I'd overlooked the
most obvious suspect, and found myself hoping
to catch a glimpse of the blond woman he'd been
canoodling with. I didn't see anyone until I pulled
into the inn driveway, though.

The yoga folks were out on the lawn today, all
twisted into some kind of pretzel pose that would
probably land me in the hospital if I tried it. As I
got out of the van and opened the cooler, I scanned
them, wondering if any of them had come to the
island to settle a score with Francine. James was as
far from Willow as possible, looking sculpted and
aloof. Next to him was Kellie, resplendent in pink
spandex, grouped with Barbara Sue and Blue. Ravi
was at the far end, away from Kellie. Sebastian and
Gage were next to each other, both looking a bit
wobbly, and Virginia and Andrew had staked out
a corner. They seemed to be getting along, I was
glad to see.

They all looked completely innocent, but any
one of them could be a murderer. I knew next to
nothing about them. And a lot of them came from
Florida.

I grabbed several bags and headed toward the kitchen door, deep in thought. Gus said Francine had made a lot of people angry. Angry enough to follow her to Cranberry Island?

After putting up the groceries—I was making avocados stuffed with crab salad for dinner... yum—I made a cup of tea, grabbed my laptop, and started typing in names.

First on the list? Francine Hodges.

I typed in Francine's name and the city she came from, and pages of results popped up immediately. Few of them were flattering.

Francine was no stranger to problems with civic organizations, it seemed. Nor was she a stranger to remaking a town to suit her vision. She'd run for councilwoman in Pompano Beach, running a nasty smear campaign against her opponent. So nasty, in fact, that she'd been sued for libel.

It hadn't stopped her from winning the election, though; her muckraking campaign had worked, and she'd managed to push through a shopping center instead of a park before she was ousted from the council on ethics charges.

I looked back at the libel campaign, wondering if maybe Francine's opponent had been angry enough to follow her up to Cranberry Island and finish the job. Her name was Audrey Meadows, a thirtysomething environmentalist who'd fought to keep Francine from letting the park be developed. She'd not only lost her libel suit, but evidently the race as well. I looked through the few pictures of her available; she was an attractive woman, and she seemed familiar, somehow, but unless she'd undergone some major plastic surgery,

she didn't resemble any of the yoga retreat participants. In one photo she was with a buff man—her
boyfriend, I guessed, based on the way they stood
together—but he was wearing sunglasses and a hat,
so I couldn't tell much about him. I searched to
see if she was married but found no reference to
a husband.

When I felt I'd exhausted that trail, I Googled
Francine again, wondering about the arson attempt
Gus had told me about. I quickly found an article.

About eight months ago, someone had doused
the Hodges' Florida garage with kerosene and set
it alight. The fire alarm had gone off, and the fire
department had limited the damage. Although no
one was arrested, Audrey Meadows's name came
up in another small article as a potential suspect.
I bookmarked the page and searched for anything
else on the topic but came up empty.

For the next twenty minutes, I went through the
other names on the inn's guest list, including the
Texan trio—I wasn't surprised to learn that Kellie had been Miss Teen Texas in high school—but
none of them were connected with Francine in
any way—or at least not any way that showed up
online.

Frustrated, I clicked back to Audrey Meadows,
trying to place her face. It was tickling the back of
my brain, but I just couldn't get it.

Finally, I closed the laptop and picked up the
phone. Charlene answered on the second ring.

"What's up?" she asked.

"I'm still trying to figure out what happened
to Francine," I said as I grabbed radishes, peppers,
and cucumbers from the fridge. I figured I'd prep

tonight's dinner while I talked with Charlene. As I chopped up veggies and transferred them to a big bowl, I told her what I'd discovered about Audrey Meadows and the development in Florida.

"Francine certainly was consistent," Charlene said.

I rinsed several baby cucumbers and transferred them to a cutting board. "I know. I recognize Audrey's face, but I can't place it. Can you pull her up and see what you think?"

"Hang on," Charlene said. A moment later, she said, "I found a picture of her at the beach. Pink T-shirt, right?"

"That's the photo," I said as I diced the cucumbers.

"I don't recognize her."

"I have a question," I said, "but promise you won't say anything to anyone." I slid the diced cucumbers into the bowl and reached for two red bell peppers.

"My lips are sealed."

"What do you know about Ingrid and her husband?" I asked as I cut into the first pepper.

"Why?"

I glanced around the kitchen, which was silly, because I was alone; still, I dropped my voice. "I saw Gus with a woman today. I'm pretty sure it was Ingrid."

"What?"

"In the woods, not far from the dock. I'm not a hundred percent sure it was her, but how many blondes are there on Cranberry Island?" I discarded the pepper tops and shook the seeds into the sink.

"I can count them on one hand," she said. "Catherine's one of them."

"I thought of her," I said as I started dicing the peppers. "But she's seeing Murray and that guy from the mainland; I don't think it's her. Anyway, if it *is* Ingrid, I think she and Gus are seeing each other."

"Gus Hodges? Having an affair?"

"Shh!"

"Lighten up. I'm in the back room."

"With Alex?"

"No," she said. "He's off taking pictures. Again."

I finished dicing the peppers and added them to the bowl with the cucumbers, then reached for the radishes and rinsed them in the sink. "I'm so sorry, Charlene."

"I just have to get used to it, I guess. Maybe my standards are too high."

I whacked off the green tops of the radishes. "They're not too high."

"Are you sure? I just... I had this fantasy... but no, never mind."

I set to work dicing radishes, letting some of my frustration with Alex fuel me, and slid the red and white chunks into the bowl. "This fantasy that your boyfriend would want to spend as much time as possible with you?"

"Yeah," she said. "That."

I grabbed a sweet onion from the basket and cut off the ends, then discarded the skin. "It's not a fantasy. He's only here for a few days; I think it's a reasonable expectation."

"You do? He's not even having dinner with me tonight," she confessed. "He's going out on a nighttime photography trip with some guy from

Mount Desert Island. They're trying to catch seals in the moonlight or something."

"And he didn't invite you?"

"Nope."

"Talk to him about it," I said as the knife cut through the onion. "If he can't make you a priority, he's not worth your time."

"But who else am I going to find to date?"

"You know," I said, "if you have to take a part-time job in Portland, do it. I hate to sound like a broken record, but I really think you need to go online to see if you can meet someone closer to home."

" It just seems so... I don't know."

"I know." I slid the onions into the bowl, admiring the bright colors of the fresh, diced vegetables, then retrieved cilantro and a couple of limes from the fridge. "But you live on an island. How else are you going to mingle?"

She sighed. "Maybe I will. I just... I just feel sort of heartbroken over Alex. It's silly, I know... we didn't even spend that much time together."

"You had a lot invested in him emotionally," I said as I rinsed the cilantro and laid it on the cutting board.

"I'm still not sure I'm ready to move on," she warned me.

"I get that," I said as I chopped the cilantro. "But it might be nice to remind yourself that he's not the only man in the world. And hopefully," I added, "you can do it without moving to Portland."

She sighed. "It's no wonder really if Ingrid did get mixed up with Gus. I mean, ninety percent of the men on this island smell like herring!"

"She is married," I reminded her.

"I know," she said. "But now that I think of it, she had perked up since the Hodges moved to the island. Actually... you know what? I'll bet they *are* having an affair."

I slid the cilantro into the bowl of chopped veggies, then added the cooked crabmeat from the tub in the fridge. "Why do you say that?"

"I think they knew each other in college. Gus was in here one day, picking up milk and eggs, and Ingrid walked in... and he recognized her. They both went to Bowdoin."

To finish the salad, I halved a couple of limes and squeezed them over everything, topping it all off with a dollop of olive oil and some salt and pepper before wrapping up the bowl and tucking it into the fridge. I'd slice the avocados just before dinner, adding a scoop of crab salad to each half. "Do you think Ingrid's the reason the Hodgeses moved to Cranberry Island?" I asked as I worked.

"I can't see Francine picking it," Charlene said. "And I don't think Gus had a lot of say."

"He didn't seem to have an opportunity to say much of anything," I said, closing the fridge. "Still, it's the only explanation I can think of for why the Hodges ended up here. He did say the isolation of the place was a plus, after the death threats."

"Death threats?"

I rinsed the cutting board in the sink as I spoke. "They got them in Florida, and here, too. I can't believe I didn't tell you!"

"What kind of threats?"

"On postcards sent from Bar Harbor—at least the ones from here were from Bar Harbor," I said.

"I don't know about the ones in Florida."

"Did Gus give them to the investigators?"

"No," I said.

"Weird."

"I thought so, too." I dried the cutting board and wiped down the counter. "I kind of razzed him about it today. Do you think maybe Ingrid got mixed up in things?"

"You mean she sent the threatening letters?"

"That would explain why he was worried about giving them to the police," I said as I finished tidying up the kitchen.

"Do you think... do you think maybe Ingrid did in Francine?"

"She's gone to some lengths for people she loved in the past," I mused. "It's entirely possible. Maybe she was just angry, and it all went wrong?"

"Maybe Ingrid was supposed to meet Gus for an assignation and Francine showed up instead."

I gazed out the window in the direction of the co-op. "He was standing on the beach, in just the same place, before he went through the woods to meet Ingrid."

"I can't believe Ingrid might be a murderer," Charlene breathed.

"Hold on there," I said. "Most of the yoga retreat is from Florida. There's a good chance one of them was involved; after all, someone sent threats when they lived in Florida, too. Plus, she died only hours after turning up at the inn."

"Why would that be?"

"Maybe she recognized someone. Maybe whoever it was was afraid she'd go to the police, and that's why the murder happened that night."

"But why was she by the co-op?" Charlene asked.

"That's a very good question," I said. "I may have to go ask her that myself."

"She could be a murderer," Charlene reminded me. "Maybe it was Ingrid who attacked the goats, not Francine."

"She does hate the goats," I said.

"All I'm saying is, be careful."

Charlene was right. I hated to think of Ingrid being a killer, but I couldn't rule it out.

"I'll figure something out," I said. As I spoke, the back door opened, and John walked in. "Gotta run... catch you later?"

"Anytime, Nat."

As I hung up, John slung himself into one of the kitchen chairs.

"You look kind of glum," I said.

"You could say that," he told me. "They just charged Claudette with murder."

CHAPTER SEVENTEEN

I SAT DOWN ACROSS FROM HIM, feeling deflated. I'd known it was probably coming—after all, she was in custody—but it was still a gut punch. "Have you talked to the detectives?"

He nodded. "No alibi. A threat. I think the knife in Francine's hand clinched it for motive."

"I knew it," I said. "Still... why would Claudette have left the goats there if they were wounded?"

"I asked that. They said it seemed like a lot of work for someone her age to corral the goats and lug that tire around. They may downgrade it to manslaughter, but still..."

"It's still a lot of time. Meanwhile, whoever really did it is free to murder again. Do they think she's connected to what happened to Rainy?"

"They're calling that an accident caused by a Klonopin overdose," he said.

"I'm not buying it."

"Me neither," he said. "Any news here?"

"A bit," I said, and told him what I'd seen in the woods near the co-op.

He gaped at me. "Ingrid and Gus? Seriously?"

"They went to Bowdoin together a long time ago. Charlene said Ingrid's been looking particularly spiffy lately. I'm not sure she was the one I saw with Gus—I only saw her from behind—but there aren't that many blondes on the island, so that's the working theory."

"Ingrid Sorenson. The keeper of island mores, breaking her wedding vows. But with Gus Hodges?"

"We don't know that for sure," I reminded him. "And men aren't exactly thick on the ground here; Charlene complains about that all the time." I'd gotten lucky, though, I thought, drinking in the handsome specimen across the table from me. "Besides, you and I both know love is blind. I mean, look at Catherine and Murray."

"I think the blinders are totally off on that one," John said.

"Uh-oh."

"I heard them arguing earlier. He's said either they're exclusive or he's done."

"What did she say?" "She didn't," he said.

As he spoke, Catherine walked in. She looked at John and narrowed her eyes. He looked like a ten-year-old boy who had just been caught with his hand in the cookie jar. "Are you talking about me?" she asked.

"We were just wondering about your new beau," I replied for him.

"You were wondering what happened between Murray and me, too, I'm guessing," she said, pulling up a chair at the table. "What happened is, I don't like the way he does business."

"Are you talking about the deal he was doing with Francine... the pier project?"

She nodded. "Values are important to me. I didn't

like this island when we came here years ago," she said, looking at John, "but I've become quite fond of it." She glanced over her shoulder. "Murray was trying to push people into bad decisions," she said. "I didn't like it. He said that's how business is done. I said if that's how business is done, I want no part of it... or him."

"And where does Nicholas come in?" I asked.

"Ah, Nicholas. Originally, he was just... I don't know." She shrugged. "To make Murray jealous, I guess. To try to bribe him in my own way, I have to confess." She blushed a little. "But the thing is, I really like him."

I could see why. He was handsome, attentive, and, if his yacht was any indication, not in any danger of going to the poorhouse. Certainly, at least from external appearances, he seemed like a step up from Murray.

"Do you know what you're going to do?" I asked.

"No," she said. "But I told Murray I wouldn't see him if he had anything to do with the pier."

"What did he say?"

"That it was business," she said.

"That doesn't bode well," I replied.

She grimaced. "That's what I thought."

"I have a question on another topic," I said, thinking of Ingrid. "But you can't tell anyone I asked."

"My lips are sealed," she said. "What is it?"

"I know you and Ingrid have had coffee a couple of times," I told her.

"We have," she agreed. "Largely talking about the pier. She was against it, and I was on her side. She was also angry at Francine Hodges for coming in and stirring everything up. She felt that outsiders should live here for a while before trying to put their stamp on things." She looked pensive. "I kind of agree with her, now." She blinked. "But what about her?"

"Did you know that she and Gus Hodges were at school together?"

"No," she said, looking surprised. "Ingrid never mentioned that." My mother-in-law pursed her lips. "She did say how sorry she felt for him, though. How hard it must be to live under a tyrant like Francine."

John and I exchanged glances.

"Why?" Catherine asked.

"I think I saw them today," I told her. "Gus and Ingrid."

"Wait," Catherine said. "Together?"

I nodded. "They were in the woods by the co-op," I told her. "Has she said anything about her own marriage?"

Catherine shook her head. "Not really. Only... well, only that she and her husband didn't spend a lot of time together." She smiled. "She told me once she was a little jealous of Murray and me. That their idea of a romantic night was watching *Jeopardy!* with the lights off."

I choked back a laugh and glanced at John. "Well, lately, ours seem to involve doing dishes and keeping our guests from throttling each other."

"Still more exciting than *Jeopardy!*" John added. "Plus, the company is riveting."

I blushed. Catherine ignored John's comment.

"Do you really think Ingrid might have something to do with what happened to Francine?"

"If Ingrid was seeing Gus, it's possible."

"You think she killed her out of jealousy?"

"I don't like to think it, but between that and Francine's determination to move the pier..." I shrugged.

"Aren't there any suspects in this yoga retreat of yours?" Catherine asked.

"A lot of them are from Florida," John commented.

"I can't find any connection between the participants and Francine, but I do know she was getting death threats in Florida," I said. "And according to one of the papers, someone tried to burn her house down."

"What?" John asked.

"They only succeeded in torching the garage."

"She was carrying a lighter when she died," John said thoughtfully. "Doesn't it seem suspicious that only the garage was lit? And that it was caught before the house went up in flames?"

"Are you suggesting Francine tried to burn down her own house?" I asked. "Why?"

"What did the article say?" John asked.

"Well, she claimed it was a woman who had tried to keep her from developing a piece of land..." I paused. "Wait. The co-op was trying to keep the pier from happening."

"But if it was her, the modus operandi is different," Catherine said. "In Florida, she set fire to her own house—assuming she was the one who did it. And here, she's attacking the co-op. If that was her intention, which is kind of hard to say. All she had was a lighter."

"The co-op is built of wood and soaked with old gasoline," John pointed out. "It wouldn't take much."

"That's true," I said, "but it's still far-fetched. There were threats against her, though, and someone spray-painted the back of the Hodges' house. I guess it could be Francine who did it. But why?"

"It sounds like she liked to stir controversy," Catherine said. "She certainly stirred things up here."

"I still think it's a stretch," I said. "But I do believe she was linked with someone at the retreat."

"Why?" Catherine asked.

"She came over to file charges against Claudette the evening before she died. But once she saw the retreat participants, she seemed to kind of cut things short and leave in a hurry."

"That does seem suggestive," John agreed.

"The thing is, the only person I can come up with who might have had a motive is a woman named Audrey Meadows, and she's not here."

"Could it be someone associated with her?" John asked.

I shook my head. "I have no idea," I told him. "I feel like we're jousting at windmills here."

He sighed. "I just wish we had some way to help Claudette."

"Me too," I said. "And I think it's time to talk to Ingrid."

"Today?" he asked.

"I've got the crab salad prepped for dinner," I told him. "Would you cover for me here?"

"Yes, but are you sure you don't want company?"

"I think she'll be more likely to talk to me woman to woman," I said.

"I don't like you going to talk to her alone,

though," he said. "She could be a murderer."

"My gut tells me she isn't. I'll take my phone with me," I said. "I'll call you when I go in."

"I still don't like it," he said. "But I know better than to try to stop you."

Ingrid's house had recently been repainted a fresh white with sleek gray shutters. The geraniums on the porch were ringed with chicken wire now, but they still looked embattled; a few stalks had been chewed off, and one side of the pot by the door looked like it had had a run-in with a drunkard wielding hedge clippers. I loved Claudette, but Ingrid was right; her goats could be a menace.

I knocked on the front door, and Ingrid appeared a moment later, wearing a blue top the same color as the one I'd seen in the woods. Although she didn't usually wear makeup, today she had on a touch of pink lipstick and some mascara. My heart sank; it looked like my suspicions were correct.

"Natalie. What are you doing out here?" she asked, looking surprised.

"We hadn't visited in a while," I said. "I thought I'd drop by to say hello."

"Come in," she said, opening the door wider. "I'll put on a cup of tea." I stepped through and followed her through the tastefully decorated living room toward the kitchen. I sat down at her antique kitchen table as she filled a blue teakettle and put it on the stove.

"Where's your husband today?" I asked, hoping she'd tell me he wasn't in the house.

She rolled her eyes. "He's out fishing, of course.

It's all he does anymore."

"Ah," I said, wondering how to broach a delicate subject. "You two have been married a long time, haven't you?"

"Since the dawn of time," she replied. "Assam tea okay?"

"Sounds good. Can I help?" I asked as she busied herself laying shortbread cookies out on a plate.

"I've got it," she told me as she set the plate on the table.

"Any news on the pier business?" I asked

"It's on hold," she said. "Although I doubt it will go through. Even though Murray's on board, I know Gus isn't a big fan of the project."

She'd given me the opening I was hoping for. "I hear you and Gus went to school together."

Her eyes widened a bit, and she froze with a tea bag in her hand. "We did," she said lightly, looking away from me. "Funny how coincidences happen! It was a long time ago, though."

"Did you know each other well at school?" I asked.

She shook her head and picked up two teacups. "Not really."

"So you just became close here on the island, then," I said.

She dropped the teacups. One of them just rolled around on the floor, but the other shattered. "Oh, no," she said, her hand over her mouth, and hurried to the pantry to retrieve a broom and dustpan.

I scooped up the intact cup as she swept up the shards.

"We're not close," she protested.

"I saw you and Gus today," I told her. "In the

woods close to the pier."

"I... we were talking about the plans for the lobster co-op," she stammered, her face red. She wouldn't meet my eye.

"I saw you kiss him," I said. She stared at the floor. I put a hand on her arm. "I'm not going to say anything to your husband. That's for you two to work out. I just want to know if maybe you know anything else about what might have happened to Francine... if Gus said something to you that he wouldn't have said to me, or to the police."

She stood there for a moment, eyes closed. Although she was completely still, I could feel the struggle going on inside her. After a moment, her shoulders slumped, and she wrapped her arms around her body. "He wanted me to get a divorce," she said abruptly, looking at the floor. "Oh, God." She went from beet red to pale, but still didn't meet my eyes. "I can't believe I'm telling you this. Promise me you won't say anything to anyone. Please."

"I promise," I said, taking the broom and dustpan from her. "Sit down," I told her as the kettle started whistling. "I'll take care of the tea."

"I feel like such a horrible, horrible person," she said, tears running down her face as she sat at the table. She reminded me of a crushed flower. "I never meant for it to happen. When he told me they were moving up here, I never thought..."

"So he was in touch with you before they moved?"

She nodded. "We connected on an alumni group online," she said.

"Were you lovers in college?"

"Only once," she said, still not meeting my eye.

"I started dating Jack at around the same time, and things between Gus and me just kind of never got started. I think he was carrying a torch for me all these years. And now, after all this time, it seems..." She shrugged and looked up at me, her eyes hollow. "Well, it's hard to choose for the rest of your life when you're only twenty-one, isn't it?"

"I can imagine it would be," I said. "So it was Gus's idea to move to Cranberry Island?"

She nodded. "He talked Francine into it. Said with all the threats, they should move somewhere far away. Somewhere that was hard to get to, where outsiders would be noticed."

"Like a gated community of sorts."

"Exactly," she said. "She read one of those *Coastal Living* articles about islands, and she agreed... but only if she could pick and completely redesign the house."

"But the whole time he just wanted to be close to you," I said.

"I didn't realize how much I meant to him," she said. "Or how much he means to me." She looked up at me. "I feel... alive, Natalie. For the first time in years. I feel alive."

I had a very bad feeling about how all this was going to turn out—anyone as crafty as Gus wasn't good news in my book—but I held my peace. "You mentioned he wanted you to get a divorce. Was he taking steps in that direction, too?"

"He said he'd talked to an attorney," she said. "There was some issue with the estate... it was complicated."

Complicated. Well, now that Francine was out of the way, there was no need to do anything legal at all. Just get the death certificate signed, and Gus was free to do what he liked. As I looked at Ingrid, whose eyes were sparkling, that very bad feeling came back. Gus Hodges's wife had come to a rather untimely end.

I was afraid Ingrid's husband might be next.

CHAPTER EIGHTEEN

I WAS BACK AT THE INN and stewing over Ingrid and Gus when the phone rang. It was Charlene.

"How's the investigation going?" she asked as I finished cutting up shallots and garlic for lobster bisque. I pushed the garlic aside and reached for an onion.

"I keep finding out all kinds of things," I said, "but I'm not sure any of them are helping me figure out what happened to Francine or Rainy."

"How's Rainy doing?"

"No change, from what I hear," I told her. I finished chopping the onion, then poured a bit of olive oil into a pan and turned on a burner. I figured I'd make the bisque now and let the flavors meld in the fridge for a few hours. "How are things with you?"

"Better, actually," she said. "Now that Alex is done with his assignment, he's been great. He's taking me out to dinner on MDI this evening, and he's been really attentive."

"Still looking for jobs in Portland?" I asked as I added the onions, garlic, and shallot to the hot oil in the pan, inhaling the savory scent. As they cooked, I grabbed the rest of the ingredients, then deglazed the pan with wine.

"No," she said, "but I'm thinking about that online dating thing."

When the wine was sizzling, I added Worcestershire sauce, Tabasco, and thyme. "Good," I said, then added a dollop of sherry. The kitchen smelled heavenly, and I hadn't even added the lobster broth yet.

"That doesn't mean I'm giving up on Alex, though. I'm just thinking about it. Plus, it might be nice to explore the area a little more, you know?"

"I like that idea," I said, retrieving lobster broth from the fridge and hurrying back to give the pan another stir.

"There's a cute guy at your retreat, too," she said. "That guy James... think he might consider a return visit to Maine?"

"You don't want to take up with James," I said.

"Why?" she asked.

"Well, if you enjoy long conversations involving lectins and dietary restrictions, go for it. But he broke up with Willow a week ago and still came on the retreat." As I spoke, I added the broth and a bit of paprika to the pan, then stirred in tomato paste and a couple of bay leaves. I'd let it simmer for ten minutes, then add cream and the extra lobster meat I'd picked the night we served lobster. Cream was low carb, right? How could my guests complain?

"That's got to be miserable for her!" Charlene said. "Why?"

"I saw her journal when I was tidying... apparently, he was still interested in someone else, I think. I'm not quite sure."

I gave the pan another stir as it came to a simmer, then turned the heat down. "So that's why he broke up with her?"

"I think so," I said. "I'm not really sure. I know she's upset, though." I thought again of the picture in James's room. Something about it was familiar... and suddenly, I thought I knew why. "I think I know who she is," I said.

I grabbed my laptop and pulled up a name, then clicked on photos until I found the right one. "That's her," I said.

"Who?"

"The woman in the picture upstairs. In his room."

"What about her?" Charlene asked.

"It's Audrey Meadows. She's the one who tangled with Francine in Florida," I said. "They argued over a development. Francine had her arrested for arson."

"I'd say the odds of that being a coincidence are low."

"I'd agree," I said. "Willow said his ex-fiancée died... hang on a moment." I typed in her name and "obituary." A chill ran through me; she'd passed six months ago. "She did die," I breathed. "And she was only thirty-five."

"That's young," Charlene said. "What was the cause of death?"

"It doesn't say," I said. "Which means it probably wasn't foul play. Or if it was, it was well hidden."

"Maybe Willow knows," Charlene said. "I think you might want to talk to her. Find out what else she knows about James. It's a shame..."

"What?"

"All the good-looking ones turn out to be messed up."

"Even Alex?"

"I don't know," she said. "I'm reserving judgment. Now, go find Willow and ask her about James. And let me know what you find out."

"Got it," I said. Had I been wrong about Gus? Was the murderer at the inn after all?

I finished the lobster bisque with cream and lobster meat and tucked it into the fridge before hunting down the yoga instructor. Willow was just finishing up a session when I found her out on the back lawn. James, as usual, was checking his Fitbit and syncing it up with his phone. "Can I talk with you for a moment?" I asked in a low voice.

"Is everything okay?" she asked, looking concerned.

"I think so," I said. "I just found something out, and I wanted to ask you about it."

"Sure," she said, and followed me into the kitchen. I opened my computer and showed her the picture of Audrey Meadows.

"Why do you have a picture of James's fiancée?" she asked, looking puzzled... and a little bit wary.

"She got into a turf war with Francine Hodges back in Florida," I told her. "Did you know anything about that?"

"Maybe," she said vaguely, shaking her head. "All I know is that she died."

"Do you know what happened?"

She shook her head again, and her eyes slid away from me. "I have a feeling it might have been suicide, actually. James never talked about it, but he let on that she struggled with depression."

"She died about six months after being charged with arson and losing the election to Francine. Think it could be related?"

She turned to face me, and her voice was somber. "Are you thinking James came here to get back at Francine for what happened to Audrey?"

"You know him better than I do," I said. "Does that sound like something he'd do?"

"He's just so... clinical," she said, her voice agitated. "I don't know. I thought I knew him, but... I just don't know anymore."

"Was he still hung up on her?" I asked gently.

Tears filled her eyes, and she looked away. "Yes," she said. "And to be honest... I wonder if he was just using me to get to Cranberry Island." She looked back at me. "I knew about his ex and Francine. He was at the yoga studio when he lost his fiancée; she came to the studio a couple of times, too, before she... passed. I didn't know Francine had moved here until she marched into the inn that night, though... and then I wondered."

"Wondered?" I prompted.

"James had been so pushy about having the retreat here. I mean, it's a lovely place, but it just seemed... weird to me."

"So you thought he pushed you to have it here just so he could get to the island with the group?"

She nodded, eyes tearing up. "And then he broke up with me last week. He was so matter-of-fact about it. I really fell for him, and now I'm wondering if he ever felt anything for me at all, or if he was just using me."

I put my hand on her arm. "I'm so sorry," I said gently. "And I hate to ask this... but do you think it's possible he killed Francine?"

"I do," she blurted out. "And it's been eating me up all week. I know someone left the inn the night she died; I was sitting by the window and I saw the flashlight. I've been worried sick and haven't known what to do."

"When did he come to Maine?"

"He flew up early," she said. "Why?"

"Francine and Gus apparently received threatening notes the week before she died," I said. "Someone sent them from Bar Harbor."

"Oh my God. You're thinking he came up early and made up the notes, then showed up at the yoga retreat so he could kill her and have someone on the island take the blame?"

"It's a theory," I said. A theory that was becoming stronger by the moment.

"I dated a murderer," she said, paling.

"We don't know that yet," I said, "but it's definitely a possibility. I think it's time we talked to the police, don't you?"

"I can't right now," she said, glancing at the clock. "I've got to run the retreat. But can you get in touch with them?"

"I will," I said. "Be careful in the meantime, okay?" As I spoke, the phone rang. Willow excused herself to go back to the retreat as I answered it.

"Rainy's coming to." It was John.

"Has she said anything?"

"Not yet," he told me.

"I just talked with Willow," I told him. "I think James may be a murderer."

"What?"

I relayed what we'd discussed. "I told her to talk to the police... but she's busy with the retreat."

"I'll call them right now and get someone over there," he said.

"I have to head to the mainland this afternoon to pick up a few things," I said. "I think I may stop by the hospital to see how Rainy's doing."

"I'll take care of dinner," he said.

"Thanks. Crab salad and lobster bisque are made; if you just throw together a salad, we'll be good."

"Are you taking the mail boat or the skiff?"

I looked at the sky; it was a beautiful clear blue. "I'll take the skiff," I said.

"Storm's coming," he warned me, "but not till tonight. Leave the skiff there and take the mail boat if it looks bad."

"Thanks," I said, grateful to have such a sweet husband.

Everyone else's relationships might be going south, but John and I were still solid. More than solid. Despite the horrible events of the week, I found myself smiling as I grabbed my jacket and headed out the back door.

The trip to the mainland was brisk and refreshing, as always. As the little boat skipped over the waves, I took a deep breath of the salt-laced air and looked back at the inn. The weathered gray shingles were accented with pale blue shutters, and the inn was nestled into the green island like a jewel. Brilliant purple lobelia and red geraniums burst from the window boxes; somehow, they'd escaped the attentions of Muffin and Pudge, at least so far. It was a far cry from my previous life as a cubicle denizen in Austin, Texas. I sometimes missed the breakfast tacos, but lobster bisque was more than a fair trade.

As I rounded the island, the lighthouse came into view. All this time I'd thought it might be responsible for what had happened to Francine... apparently, I'd been wrong. I'd also been wrong about Gus; I'd thought him mild-mannered and completely subjugated to his powerful wife. Ingrid, too, had surprised me. You never could tell with people, could you?

I wound through a colorful array of buoys, most of them familiar, and thought of the quiet lobster-ing territory war that was happening once again on the island... under cover of night. The island might look peaceful, but lots of things were hap-pening on Cranberry Island this summer... and a lot of them were rather surprising.

Had James sent the letters from Bar Harbor? I wondered. And had the flashlight I'd seen leaving the inn been him on his way to kill Francine... or spray-paint a threatening message on her house? What was the purpose of sending those threatening letters, anyway? To scare her? I was guessing that was part of it... but I suspected he was also trying to throw suspicion off himself. I knew there had been articles about Francine in the *Daily Mail* recently; it wouldn't take too much Googling to discover she was up to her old tricks again on Cranberry Island. And by showing up with the yoga retreat, James wouldn't stand out as much on the island as a solo visitor; he was just one of the pack.

Had he really used Willow to get to the island? And if I was right, and he was the killer, why had he hurt Rainy?

As the mainland grew closer, I slowed the skiff; soon, I was weaving through the beautiful sailboats moored in Northeast Harbor. I tied up at the dock and then headed to the little Kia John and I kept on the mainland, hoping the battery hadn't died. My next stop was the hospital... and Rainy.

Rainy was on the second floor of the hospital, according to the volunteer at the front desk. I headed upstairs with the flowers I'd picked up on the way in hand, hoping the young woman would be conscious... and that her prognosis was good.

"Can I help you?" asked the nurse at the station closest to her room.

"I'm looking for Rainy," I said.

"Oh, she's in there," the nurse said. "Visiting with her uncle."

"I didn't realize she had family in town!" I said. Ravi and Willow hadn't mentioned anyone coming to visit. I hesitated; the door was closed.

"I'm sure it's fine if you go in," she said.

I opened the door; the curtain was closed around Rainy, and other than the sound of breathing, I couldn't hear anything. I closed the door behind me and took a few steps forward. "Hello?"

Somebody swore. I stepped around the curtain and encountered a man holding a syringe in his hand.

It was Gus Hodges.

"What are you doing here?" I asked. "And what

are you doing with that syringe?"

He fumbled at his waistband; a moment later, I was staring into the barrel of a gun.

CHAPTER NINETEEN

"SHUT UP," HE SAID. "JUST... shut up." He swept a hand over what was left of his hair, looking spooked. "I knew I should have taken care of this days ago."

"Taken care of... of Rainy? Wait a moment." Suddenly, it all fit together. Meeting Ingrid in secret by the co-op and pushing for her to be divorced. Not sharing the threatening notes with the police. Forty years of living with Francine... I almost felt sorry for him.

Almost.

"You killed Francine," I said slowly, scanning the room and trying to figure out how to get out of here alive. What would he do if a nurse walked in? Kill all three of us? I just didn't know, so I kept talking. "You wanted to be with Ingrid, so you killed your wife."

"Don't get Ingrid into this!" he said.

"Did she follow you?" I asked. "When you went out to meet Ingrid... I presume that's where you were going. Did she catch you?"

"I wasn't meeting Ingrid," he said. "I would never get her involved in something like this."

Plus, who would want to run off with a murderer?

"What was Francine doing there?"

"She was going to set the co-op on fire," he said. "I followed her there."

"What?"

"She figured if they wouldn't listen to her, she'd send the place up in flames. She had her eye on the pier, too. She was a bit of a firebug."

"Was she responsible for the fire in Florida, too?"

He nodded. "That's why she only set the garage on fire. She could blame the other woman, get the insurance money, and keep the house."

"Nice," I said, hoping the nurse would come soon. Very soon. I scanned the room; the Call button was out of sight, probably buried in the blankets. Rainy's face was peaceful: no help to be found there. "That explains the lighter," I said, trying to buy some time. "And the goats?"

He shrugged. "I always carry a pocket knife. They were there... it was convenient. Bolstered the motive."

"And then you left the knife next to Francine. Smart."

"I wiped the handle, of course," he said, puffing up a little bit.

"And Rainy?"

"She knew," he said. "She saw me that night, when I was walking home."

"You tried to kill her just because she saw you?"

"I was afraid she'd say something. I couldn't take the risk; I had to be sure."

"So you wrote the notes," I said.

He nodded. "So it would look like Florida. And then, when Claudette attacked Francine in the convenient store... the timing was perfect, anyway."

"You were planning it, then. It wasn't an accident."

"It wasn't," he said. "I always wanted to be with Ingrid. And she wants to be with me. I should have married her instead, all those years ago, but Francine..."

"What happened?" I asked, edging closer to the bed. He was holding the gun in one hand and the syringe in the other. What was in the syringe? I wondered. Nothing good, I was sure of that.

"She decided I was the one. I was weak. And before I knew it, we were engaged to be married." He shrugged. "She was a force of nature. I was kind of surprised the brick worked."

I could see that, but didn't feel it was the moment to discuss it. I took another step closer to the bed... and Rainy, whose face was still and pale. "Out of curiosity... what do you know about Audrey Meadows? The woman Francine framed for arson?"

"Oh, her. Yes... Francine wasn't very happy with her. She cost her a lot in legal fees."

"So she committed arson on her own house to get her arrested?"

"Of course she did," Gus said. "Sent the letters and everything... at least at first. That's what gave me the idea to do it here."

"So *you* sent the threatening notes?"

"I did... and boy, was she unhappy about that. Not used to things being turned against her."

"Why did she decide to move to Maine?" I asked.

"I wanted her to," he said. "I started sending notes in Florida. And then I slashed her tires. It wasn't hard to convince her to get out of town.

And when I told her about how isolated the island was..." He shrugged. "Imagine her surprise when she started to get letters here, too."

"It's like you enjoyed it."

"I kind of did. I spent so many years dancing to her tune, it was a nice change of pace. Plus, I got my second chance with Ingrid."

"Did Francine know about it?"

He shrugged. "She was too self-involved, I think."

"Why not just divorce her?"

He blinked at me. "And be penniless? After all the years I put up with her? I don't think so."

"How could you have been penniless?"

"She's got good attorneys. Always used them, and never let me forget where the money came from." He grimaced. "Take no prisoners, that was her motto. Her only exception was me." His face drooped, and even though he was holding a gun on me, I felt a twinge of pity. His and Francine's seemed to have been something of a twisted relationship. It didn't excuse what he'd done... but I could at least sort of understand it.

Except for the part about killing someone. And framing a stranger for your crime.

"What happened to Audrey? Do you know?"

"Suicide," he said shortly.

So it was suicide, just as I'd suspected. Poor James. "I think her fiancé had a vendetta against your wife. He's at the retreat."

"I know," he said, smiling. "They'll never figure out it was me."

"They will if you shoot me here," I pointed out.

"Then we'll have to go somewhere else," he said. "But first..." He raised the hand with the syringe.

"What is that?"

"Air," he said.

"She's so young, though," I said, edging closer to the bed and trying to find the Call button. As he focused on the syringe, the gun wavered, pointing a little to the right of me. He was about to sink it into the line when the door opened.

He dropped the hand with the syringe, tucked the gun into his jacket—still aimed at me—and smiled at the nurse who came in.

"Still sleeping?" she asked brightly.

"Still sleeping," Gus said. "And we were just leaving," he added, making my eyebrows rise; that I hadn't expected. As he spoke, he crossed the room and stood behind me. "Time for an early dinner. Let's go!" he added in a firm but bright tone.

I probably should have made a scene right there, but I didn't, and before I knew it, he was walking me out of the hospital toward the parking lot.

"Why did you decide to leave?"

"The timing was wrong. I'll deal with you first, then go back to take care of her. I'm not sure she even saw me, but it's important to be thorough and take precautions." He stopped beside a gold Lexus, then paused. "Where's your car?" he asked.

"Over there," I said, pointing."

"We'll take yours," he said. As he continued to train the gun on me, we walked over to my Kia. "Give me the phone and get in the car," he said when we got there. I fumbled in my purse for the keys and phone, and reluctantly offered both. "Keep the keys," he told me as he grabbed my phone. "You're driving."

"Where are we going?"

"None of your business," he told me, sounding a whole lot less like the meek husband I'd thought he was the first time I'd met him.

He kept the gun trained on me as I climbed into the driver's seat. I had the urge to take off and leave him behind, but I was afraid he'd shoot me before I could get anywhere. He walked behind the car and got into the passenger seat.

"You know, you could say it was an accident," I told him. "Manslaughter. Rainy's still alive. If you don't kill her—or me—you won't be charged with multiple murders."

"Too late for that," he said. "I'm not young anymore. I don't have time to waste in jail. I lost Ingrid once; I'm not going to lose her again."

"Don't you think she's likely to bolt when she finds out what happened here?" I still hadn't started the car; I was stalling.

"She's not going to find out," he said. "In fact, no one's going to find you. Your disappearance will be just another unsolved mystery." The coldness in his voice sent shivers down my spine. "Drive," he ordered, and I turned the key in the ignition and obeyed.

He directed me to the bridge leading from Mount Desert Island to the mainland. The tide was low, and I could smell the tang of seaweed as I crossed. Would it be the last time? I wondered, feeling a kernel of fear expand in my stomach. "Where are we going?" I asked again. Not that I expected him to answer.

"You'll see," he said as I continued driving, past the little airport, past all the small businesses lining the road to the island. I glanced over at him, hoping he would drop the muzzle of the gun, but it was still aimed directly at me.

I asked him more questions, but apparently, he was done talking, and an icy silence filled the car despite the warm sunshine outside.

As we rolled into Ellsworth, I racked my brain for ideas. How was I going to get out of this? I couldn't call 911 on my phone because Gus had taken it. I had no weapons, and I felt very uncomfortable with the idea of trying to wrench a loaded gun—I presumed it was loaded—out of someone's hand when it was pointed at me. On the other hand, I was pretty sure it would be discharged soon if I didn't come up with a plan.

I was coming up empty… until we came to a traffic light in Ellsworth. I was third back from the light. Beside me on the left, back two cars, was a police cruiser.

"Just keep going straight," he said. "Don't do anything." He'd spotted it, too.

My eyes flicked to the rearview mirror. I could see the cop in the car, staring out into the distance, not paying attention to much of anything at all. I looked at the car in front of me: a brown Ford Taurus with Connecticut plates. The light turned green. It was now or never. Saying a brief, silent prayer, I slammed on the gas and rammed into the trunk of the Taurus, squeezing my eyes shut and hoping the crack I heard wasn't a gunshot.

CHAPTER TWENTY

I T WASN'T, THANKFULLY. THE AIRBAGS had deployed, and for a moment all I saw was white. Beside me, I heard something heavy hit the floor. I looked over; Gus had lost the gun. I lunged toward the passenger floorboard but stopped short; my seat belt was locked. I fumbled for the latch and released it, then strained to reach the passenger floorboard again, struggling to push the half-deflated airbag out of the way.

"Leave it alone!" Gus yelled as we both scrabbled on the floor. I didn't have time to look to see what was going on outside the car; I hoped the policeman was coming to see what was going on, but I wasn't going to count on that. My hand closed on the grip just as Gus's closed on the barrel. Adrenaline coursing through me, I yanked the gun back. There was a deafening crack and a searing pain in my leg, but I still held on to the gun. With my free hand, I fumbled for the door handle. When my fingers closed on it, I flung open the car door and threw the gun out onto the pavement, just as the policeman was walking up to the Kia.

He reached for his sidearm and took cover, pointing the gun at me. "I'm not armed," I told him, and looked down at my leg. It was covered in blood. "I've been shot," I said, and realized I could barely hear my own words. As I spoke, Gus slammed the passenger door open and vaulted out of the car. "He's a murderer," I said to no one in particular. Then, somewhere in the distance, there was another crack, and then everything went dark.

I woke up staring into a friendly face. I wasn't in the car anymore; I was lying on a stretcher. "Where am I?" I asked.

"In an ambulance," the kind woman said, her voice muffled.

It all came rushing back to me. "My leg..."

"It's going to be fine," she said. "You'll have a scar, but it didn't hit anything vital. It just bled a lot."

"Thank goodness," I said. "And Gus?"

"The gentleman in the car?" she asked.

"Him. Yes. He tried to kill me."

"He's in another ambulance," she informed me. "The officer on duty shot him when he tried to flee."

"How bad?"

"He'll live," she said as the ambulance turned into the hospital parking lot.

I was spending more time at the hospital than I liked, I thought, as the EMT opened the ambulance doors and rolled me into the building.

On the plus side, though, at least Rainy and I were still among the living.

The yoga retreat was on its last day when I got back to the inn early the next day. My leg was bandaged and I was limping, but at least I was in good enough shape to go home. The officer had shot Gus in the shoulder. Although he was still in the hospital, he'd been arrested after the incident, and I'd had a long chat with the police the night before. My ears still felt muffled, as if they were packed with cotton, and my leg still hurt, but all in all, I was in pretty good shape. Better yet, Rainy had come to long enough to confirm that Gus was the one who had attacked her as she was out walking to clear her head (she had admitted to taking a few too many Klonopin, too). The police had released Claudette, and she was back with her family. I had hobbled down to the kitchen to make myself a cup of tea when Ingrid knocked at the door, looking like she'd aged ten years in just a few days.

"Are you okay?" she asked.

"I'm fine," I said, waving at my leg. "Only a flesh wound."

"Do you have a few minutes to talk?" she asked. Her eyes were swollen and red.

"Come in," I said. "I'll make us both some tea."

"You know what happened," she said bluntly as she sat down at the kitchen table.

"I do," I said as I filled the kettle.

"I can't believe it," she said. "I loved him—or I thought I did—but I didn't want Francine to die for us to be together."

"It wasn't your fault," I reassured her as I put the kettle on the stove. I walked over to Ingrid and put a hand on her shoulder; at my touch, she began to sob.

"If I hadn't responded to him, none of this would have happened. Francine would still be alive, and I wouldn't be in this horrible, horrible situation. I can't believe what I've done... that I fell for someone like that."

"You didn't know," I told her. "It was a mistake." I wasn't comfortable condoning an affair, although it's impossible for anyone to see from the outside what goes on inside a marriage, but I did know she wasn't responsible for what Gus had done to Francine. And Rainy.

"What do I tell Jack?" she asked.

"I don't know," I told her. "I'd recommend the two of you see a counselor, see if things are salvageable."

"That's the thing," Ingrid said. "I don't know if they are salvageable."

"That's what the counselor can help you with," I said. "But you have to stop blaming yourself for what happened to Francine. There was no way for you to know he would do that."

"I should have known," she said. "If I hadn't answered that first message, none of this would have happened."

"Maybe not," I agreed, "but I suspect it would have happened in a different way. There's no way to know... but again, it's not your fault."

"I just wish I could believe that," she said.

"I'm so sorry," I told her.

She took a deep breath. "I have to tell him," she announced.

"Yes," I said. "You do. But I wouldn't do it until you're in a counselor's office."

"You think?"

"I do," I said. The teakettle started to whistle. "Black tea or herbal?" I asked.

She stood up. "Thanks, but I think I'm going to go make an appointment right now. I can't have this hanging over my head."

"You've got a lot of healing to do," I said.

"And some wounds to open, I'm afraid," she replied, looking stricken and forlorn. "The thing is... I really thought I loved him."

"I'm so sorry," I repeated, and tears welled up in her eyes.

"Thanks," she said. She swiped at her eyes and straightened up. "I guess it's time to go face the music."

"I'm here if you need to talk," I offered.

"Thank you," she said again. "I can't tell you how much that means to me."

She gave me a brief, awkward hug, then headed out the door and up the hill.

I had just poured hot water into the teapot when there was a knock at the door to the dining room. "Come in," I called.

It was Willow.

"How's it going?" I asked.

"Better," she said. "Rainy's improving, and the retreat is almost over... and I never have to see James again. But more importantly... how are *you* doing?"

"I'll be fine," I said. "Frankly, I feel a lot better now that the whole situation's been squared away."

"I know it's been tough," I said.

"Tea?" I offered.

"No, thanks," she said, smiling. "I only have a minute. I just wanted to check in with you."

"Thanks," I said as I poured myself a cup and hobbled over to the table.

"Are you sure you're going to be okay?" she asked.

"That's what they tell me," I replied. "At least I have an excuse to have people wait on me for a few days," I said with a grin.

"There is that," she said as she perched on the chair across from me. She reminded me of a bird about to take flight. "This whole week has been a disaster," she said. "Rainy and Ravi, that awful woman Kellie, and James... " She drooped a little bit as she said his name. "At least I know I wasn't seeing a murderer," she said, shuddering. "For a little while there, I thought..."

"I did, too," I said. "In fact, if I hadn't walked in on Gus about to do in Rainy, I might have told the police I thought he was the killer."

"I talked to him," she said. "I asked him point-blank if he'd asked me to set the retreat here so he could do something to Francine."

"What did he say?"

"Actually, he told me he had. He'd planned to do something... but couldn't bring himself to do it once he was here."

"I understand his fiancée committed suicide in part because of Francine."

She nodded. "She had mental health issues, obviously... but what James told me what Francine did was a trigger. He apologized to me," she said, her eyes welling up. "He told me he did have feelings for me, but... he knew it wasn't fair to me if he wasn't over Audrey."

"That was big of him," I said. "It might have been

nice for him to tell you that when he broke up."

"I think he has a hard time with feelings," she said.

"In which case, maybe it's not so bad that you broke up. I mean, Willow, you're beautiful, successful, engaging... there have to be hundreds of guys who would love to date you."

"Thanks," she said with a shy smile. "I guess... I guess I just got attached too quickly."

"It happens," I told her. "You're not the only one to get mixed up with the wrong sort."

"Like Francine," she said. "Why did he do it anyway? Her husband?"

I shrugged. What had happened between Gus and Ingrid wasn't for me to talk about. "Marriages are mysterious things," I said vaguely. "She wasn't a very nice person, but I do feel bad for her."

"I wonder about Kellie, too," she said. "If she's attacking random men at yoga retreats, things at home can't be too awesome."

"Did she go after someone else?"

"James had to fob her off last night," she said. "She was trying to get into his room."

"She's a mess," I said.

"I know. I kind of want to tell her husband, but I figure it's best to let them figure things out themselves."

"You're probably right," I said, and took a sip of my tea.

"But enough about that," Willow said, straightening up on the edge of her chair. "What do you think they're going to do about the pier now?"

"That's a good question," I said. "I imagine without a joint investor, Murray may have to table his plans."

"So there is a silver lining in all of this," she said.

"I guess you could say so. I'm just glad Rainy's okay."

"Thank goodness you walked in on him when you did," she said. "Rainy may be a bit lost, but she's a good person. I would hate to have had something happen to her."

"I'm still not sure if Ravi gave her extra Klonopin, or if she took it herself."

Willow grimaced. "I'm pretty sure it wasn't Ravi," she said. "Rainy's been struggling for a while. The yoga seemed to be working, but with all the drama with Ravi..." She sighed. "Maybe this will be what she needs to get back into treatment."

"Here's hoping," I said, taking another sip of tea.

She glanced at the clock again. "I really should go," she said. "It's almost time to walk over to the lobster pound." John had arranged for the entire retreat to eat there and give us both a break. "Are you coming?"

"I'm just going to have some leftover lobster bisque and relax on the porch, I think."

"Oh, the bisque," she said, eyes widening. "I think I'd weigh three hundred pounds if I lived here."

I eyed her superfit form and tried not to roll my eyes. "Somehow, I think you'd manage," I said, and as I took another sip of tea, she flitted back to the retreat.

I had just finished a Kate Baray mystery and was about to drift off on the back porch when I heard my name. I looked up to see John walking up from the dock, looking every bit the L.L. Bean model in his jeans, with a green Henley shirt that matched his eyes.

"How's the patient?" he asked as I raised a hand to shield my eyes from the sun.

"Taking it easy, as ordered," I said.

"That's a refreshing change of pace," he said, kissing the top of my head lightly. "It's been an exciting day on the island," he said, settling into the chair next to mine.

"Tell me," I said.

"Well, Charlene is on cloud nine since Alex surprised her by inviting her to be his companion on a two-week cruise in Alaska," he said.

"What? And she's going?"

"He apologized for his bad behavior, and she's willing to give him a second chance."

"I'm still not sure what I think of Alex, but at least maybe she won't move to Portland," I said. "Any word on Murray and the pier?"

"I talked with my mom about that just a little while ago," he said. "She and Murray are patching things up, and he's promised to let the project go."

"What happened?"

"Turns out Mr. Suave was romancing at least one other lady at the same time," he said. "My mother was leaving the grocery store in Northeast Harbor yesterday when she spotted him canoodling with one of the summer people at the bakery down the street."

"She was seeing two people, too," I pointed out.

"Actually, she wasn't," John said. "She'd told Murray they were taking a break before she started seeing the yacht guy."

"Did she? I'm glad she was honest about it."

"She called it off with him when he was being mulish about the pier. She just didn't want to rub her new beau in his face."

"That was kind of her," I said. "I'm glad she's getting things squared away." I stretched, enjoying the feel of the northern sun on my arms and legs. The parts that weren't bandaged anyway. I wondered how big a scar I'd have, then decided not to worry about it; I was lucky just to have a scar, after all. Things could have been a lot worse. "So we've got Claudette safe on the island again, Rainy's recovering, Charlene's planning on staying, and the pier project is on hold. Now the only thing we need to do is get Gwen and Adam's wedding taken care of."

"Adam told me they set a date," he said. "They're getting hitched in October, caterer or no caterer." He grinned at me. "How are you at baking wedding cakes?"

"I guess we'll find out," I said as he reached over and grabbed my hand. We were about to kiss when the sound of voices floated to us.

"Yoga retreat," John said. "Bad timing."

"We can always head inside," I said.

"I think that's an offer I can't refuse," he said with a smile that made my insides turn over, and I followed him inside, closing the door behind me.

RECIPES

Natalie's Sort-of Guiltless (Okay, Gluten-Free Anyway) Flourless Chocolate Cake

Ingredients:

½ cup water
¼ tsp. salt
¾ cup white sugar
18 (1-oz.) squares bittersweet chocolate
1 cup unsalted butter
6 eggs

Directions:

Preheat oven to 300 degrees and grease one 10-inch round cake pan; set aside. Put a kettle on to boil (you'll need water to create the water bath in which you'll bake the cake).

In a small saucepan over medium heat, combine the water, salt, and sugar. Stir until completely dissolved and set aside.

Melt the bittersweet chocolate in the microwave or a double boiler and pour it into the bowl of an electric mixer. Cut the butter into pieces and beat it into the chocolate, one piece at a time. Beat in the hot sugar water. Slowly beat in the eggs, one at a time.

Pour the batter into the prepared pan. Put the cake pan in a pan that's a few inches larger than the cake pan and fill the larger pan with boiling water, halfway up the sides of the cake pan.

Bake cake in the water bath at 300 degrees for 45 minutes. (The center will still look wet.) Chill cake in the pan overnight. To unmold, dip the bottom of the cake pan in hot water for 10 seconds and invert onto a serving plate.

Velvety Lobster Bisque

Ingredients:
2 tbs. minced shallots
2 tbs. chopped green onions
3 garlic cloves, crushed
¼ cup white wine
2 tsp. Worcestershire sauce
2 tsp. Tabasco sauce
1 tsp. dried thyme
6 tbs. dry sherry
1 tsp. paprika
1 cup lobster broth *or* 1 cup hot water and 1 tsp.
lobster base (better than bouillon)
4 oz. tomato paste
2 bay leaves
2 cups heavy whipping cream
4 tbs. butter
½ lb. lobster meat, cut into small chunks

Directions:
In a sauté pan, heat a little oil over med-high heat and sauté shallots, onions, and garlic for one minute.

Deglaze the pan with the white wine.

Add the Worcestershire, Tabasco, and thyme and sauté for another minute.

Deglaze the pan with the sherry.

Add the paprika, hot water, and lobster base and combine well.

Stir in tomato paste and add the bay leaves.

Simmer for 10 minutes.

Whisk in heavy cream and the butter and bring to a boil.

Add the lobster and simmer until cooked through.

Serve with crusty garlic bread.

Serves 2–3

Gray Whale Inn Morning Glory Muffins

Ingredients:
1¼ cups packed brown sugar
3 eggs
½ cup melted butter
1 tsp. vanilla
2 cups white whole wheat flour
2½ tsp. baking soda
½ tsp. salt
2½ tsp. cinnamon
2 cups shredded carrots
½ cup raisins
1 cup chopped apples
Optional: Turbinado sugar, for topping

Directions:
Preheat oven to 350 degrees. Line muffin tin with paper liners or spray with cooking spray.

In a large bowl, whisk together sugar, eggs, oil, butter, and vanilla.

In a separate bowl, sift together flour, baking soda, salt, and cinnamon.

Add wet ingredients to dry ingredients and stir just until combined. Do not overmix.

Fold in carrots, raisins, and apples.

Divide batter evenly among prepared muffin cups. Sprinkle with Turbinado sugar.

Bake for 20 minutes, or until toothpick inserted in center comes out clean.

Makes 12 muffins.

Crab Salad Stuffed Avocados

Ingredients:
For the crab salad:
1 lb. cooked crabmeat
½ red onion, finely chopped
½ red bell pepper, finely diced
½ green bell pepper, finely diced
½ cucumber, finely diced
4 radishes, finely diced
Juice of 2 limes
2 tbs. olive oil
2 tbs. finely chopped cilantro
Salt and pepper to taste

For the stuffed avocados:
4–5 ripe but firm avocados
½ lime
To garnish:
Lettuce or salad greens, cilantro leaves, chopped
green onions or chives, radishes

Directions:
To prepare crab salad:
Mix the cooked crabmeat with diced onions,
diced bell peppers, diced cucumbers, diced rad-
ish, lime juice, olive oil, chopped cilantro, and salt/
pepper. The salad can be prepared in advance and
kept refrigerated until just ready to assemble the
avocados.

To prepare the crab stuffed avocados:

Cut the avocados in half, remove the seeds, and peel the avocados. Sprinkle each avocado half with a little lime (or lemon) juice to prevent the avocados from browning too quickly.

Fill the center of the avocados halves with the crab salad. Serve the crab-stuffed avocados over lettuce leaves and garnished with chopped chives (or green onions) and radishes.

Eli's Lemon Cookies

Ingredients:
1 cup butter, softened
1½ cups sugar
1 egg
1 tsp. lemon juice
1 tbs. lemon zest
1 tsp. vanilla
½ tsp. salt
½ tsp. baking powder
2 cups flour

Lemon Glaze:
1½ cups powdered sugar
1 tbs. lemon juice
1 tbs. lemon zest
1 tbs. milk
¼ tsp. vanilla

Directions:
Preheat oven to 350 degrees. In a large bowl, cream butter and sugar together.

Add egg and beat in well.

Add lemon juice, lemon zest, and vanilla, and mix until well blended.

Add salt, baking powder, and flour, and mix until well incorporated.

Roll cookies into 1-inch balls and place on greased cookie sheet. Space cookie dough balls about 2 inches apart. Bake at 350 degrees for 8–10 minutes or until lightly golden on the edges of cookies.

Combine glaze ingredients in a medium bowl and whisk until smooth glaze is formed. Drizzle as much as desired over slightly warmed cookies and let finish cooling completely before eating.

Bonus Recipe:
Natalie's Favorite Popovers

<u>Tips:</u>

1) Bake on the bottom rack of your oven (with room above for them to expand).
2) Use popover pans.
3) Don't open the oven until the baking time is over.

Here's the recipe I used—it's right out of the *Jordan Pond House Cookbook* (which I highly recommend, as it includes recipes for lots of scrumptious dishes like Lobster Stew):

For 8–12 popovers

4 eggs

2 cups milk (I use 1 percent)

2 cups flour

½ tsp. salt

1/6 tsp. baking soda

(The cookbook recommends making the batter a day ahead of time, refrigerating it, and then letting it return to room temperature, but I skipped the day-before thing. I did, however, let it warm up to room temperature.)

Preheat oven to 450.

Break eggs into mixing bowl and whip; add milk and blend.

Add remaining ingredients and mix until almost

smooth; don't overbeat.

Fill greased popover pans, muffin tins, or custard cups ¾ full.

Bake for 14 minutes at 450, then reduce heat to 350 and bake 15 minutes more. (*Don't open oven until baking is complete!*) They'll be crispy brown on the outside and moist on the inside at this point; remove them from the pans and serve with butter and strawberry preserves. (Jordan Pond House uses Stonewall brand: I looked in the gift shop.)

Bonus Recipe: Blueberry French Toast

Ingredients:
12 slices day-old white bread, crusts removed
2 pkgs. (8-oz. each) cream cheese
1 cup fresh or frozen blueberries
12 large eggs, lightly beaten
2 cups 2 percent milk
⅓ cup maple syrup or honey

Sauce ingredients:
1 cup sugar
1 cup water
2 tbs. cornstarch
1 cup fresh or frozen blueberries
1 tbs. butter

Directions:
Cut bread into 1-in. cubes; place half in a greased 9 x 13-in. baking dish. Cut cream cheese into 1-in. cubes; place over bread. Top with blueberries and remaining bread cubes.

Whisk the eggs, milk, and syrup in a large bowl. Pour over bread mixture. Cover and refrigerate for 8 hours or overnight.

Remove from the refrigerator 30 minutes before baking. Cover and bake at 350 degrees for 30 minutes. Uncover; bake 25–30 minutes longer or until a knife inserted in center comes out clean.

Combine the sugar, water, and cornstarch until smooth in a small saucepan. Bring to a boil over medium heat; cook and stir until thickened, 3 minutes. Stir in blueberries; bring to a boil. Reduce heat and simmer until berries burst, 8–10 minutes. Remove from heat; stir in butter. Serve with French toast. 8 servings (1¾ cups sauce).

**TURN THE PAGE FOR A
SNEAK PEEK OF**

KILLER JAM
A DEWBERRY FARM MYSTERY

CHAPTER 1

I'VE ALWAYS HEARD IT'S NO use crying over spilled milk. But after three days of attempting to milk Blossom the cow (formerly Heifer #82), only to have her deliver a well-timed kick that deposited the entire contents of my bucket on the stall floor, it was hard not to feel a few tears of frustration forming in the corners of my eyes.

Stifling a sigh, I surveyed the giant puddle on the floor of the milking stall and reached for the hose. I'd tried surrounding the bucket with blocks, holding it in place with my feet—even tying the handle to the side of the stall with a length of twine. But for the sixth straight time, I had just squeezed the last drops from the teats when Blossom swung her right rear hoof in a kind of bovine hook kick, walloping the top of the bucket and sending gallons of the creamy white fluid spilling across both the concrete floor and my boots. I reprimanded her, but she simply tossed her head and grabbed another mouthful of the feed I affectionately called "cow chow."

She looked so unassuming. So velvety-nosed and kind, with big, long-lashed eyes. At least she had on the day I'd selected her from the line of cows for sale at the Double-Bar Ranch. Despite all the reading I'd done on selecting a heifer, when she pressed her soft nose up against my cheek, I knew she belonged at Dewberry Farm. Thankfully, the rancher I'd purchased her from had seemed more than happy to let her go, extolling her good nature and excellent production.

He'd somehow failed to mention her phobia of filled buckets.

Now, as I watched the tawny heifer gamboling into the pasture beside my farmhouse, kicking her heels up in what I imagined was a cow's version of the middle finger, I took a deep breath and tried to be philosophical about the whole thing. She still had those big brown eyes, and it made me happy to think of her in my pasture rather than the cramped conditions at Double-Bar Ranch. And she'd only kicked the milk bucket, not me.

Despite the farm's growing pains, as I turned toward the farmhouse, I couldn't help but smile. After fifteen years of life in Houston, I now lived in a century-old yellow farmhouse—the one I'd dreamed of owning my whole life—with ten acres of rolling pasture and field, a peach orchard, a patch of dewberries, and a quaint, bustling town just up the road. The mayor had even installed a Wi-Fi transmitter on the water tower, which meant I could someday put up a website for the farm. So what if Blossom was more trouble than I'd expected, I told myself. I'd only been a dairy farmer for seventy-two hours; how could I expect to know everything?

In fact, it had only been six months since my college roommate, Natalie Barnes, had convinced me to buy the farm that had once belonged to my grandparents. Natalie had cashed in her chips a few years back and bought an inn in Maine, and I'd never seen her happier. With my friend's encouragement, I'd gone after the dream of reliving those childhood summers, which I'd spent fishing in the creek and learning to put up jam at my grandmother's elbow.

It had been a long time since those magical days in Grandma Vogel's steamy, deliciously scented kitchen. I'd spent several years as a reporter for the Houston Chronicle, fantasizing about a simpler life as I wrote about big-city crime and corruption. As an antidote to the heartache I'd seen in my job, I'd grown tomatoes in a sunny patch of the backyard, made batches of soap on the kitchen stove, and even kept a couple of chickens until the neighbors complained.

Ever since those long summer days, I'd always fantasized about living in Buttercup, but it wasn't until two events happened almost simultaneously that my dream moved from fantasy to reality. First, the paper I worked for, which like most newspapers was suffering from the onset of the digital age, laid off half the staff, offering me a buyout that, combined with my savings and the equity on my small house, would give me a nice nest egg. And second, as I browsed the web one day, I discovered that my grandmother's farm—which she'd sold fifteen years ago, after my grandfather passed—was up for sale.

Ignoring my financial advisor's advice—and fending off questions from friends who questioned my sanity—I raided the library for every homesteading book I could find, cobbled together a plan

I hoped would keep me from starving, took the buyout from the paper, and put an offer in on Dewberry Farm. Within a month, I went from being Lucy Resnick, reporter, to Lucy Resnick, unemployed homesteader of my grandparents' derelict farm. Now, after months of backbreaking work, I surveyed the rows of fresh green lettuce and broccoli plants sprouting up in the fields behind the house with a deep sense of satisfaction. I might not be rich, and I might not know how to milk a cow, but I was living the life I'd always wanted.

I focused on the tasks for the day, mentally crossing cheese making off the list as I headed for the little yellow farmhouse. There might not be fresh mozzarella on the menu, but I did have two more batches of soap to make, along with shade cover to spread over the lettuce, cucumber seeds to plant, chickens to feed, and buckets of dewberries to pick and turn into jam. I also needed to stop by and pick up some beeswax from the Bees' Knees, owned by local beekeeper Nancy Shaw.

The little beeswax candles I made in short mason jars were a top seller at Buttercup Market Days, and I needed to make more.

Fortunately, it was a gorgeous late spring day, with late bluebonnets carpeting the roadsides and larkspur blanketing the meadow beside the house, the tall flowers' ruffled lavender and pink spikes bringing a smile to my face. They'd make beautiful bouquets for the market this coming weekend— and for the pitcher in the middle of my kitchen table. Although the yellow Victorian-style farmhouse had been neglected and left vacant for the past decade or more, many of my grandmother's furnishings remained. She hadn't been able to take them with her to the retirement home, and for some reason, nobody else had claimed or moved them out, so many things I remembered from my childhood were still there.

The house had good bones, and with a bit of paint and elbow grease, I had quickly made it a comfortable home. The white tiled countertop sparkled again, and my grandmother's pie safe with its punched tin panels was filled with jars of jam for the market. I smoothed my hand over the enormous pine table my grandmother had served Sunday dinners on for years. I'd had to work to refinish it, sanding it down before adding several layers of polyurethane to the weathered surface, but I felt connected to my grandmother every time I sat down to a meal.

The outside had taken a bit more effort. Although the graceful oaks still sheltered the house, looking much like they had when I had visited as a child, the line of roses that lined the picket fence had suffered from neglect, and the irises were lost in a thicket of Johnson grass. The land itself had been in worse shape; the dewberries the farm had been named for had crept up into where the garden used to be, hiding in a sea of mesquite saplings and giant purple thistles. I had had to pay someone to plow a few acres for planting, and had lost some of the extra poundage I'd picked up at my desk job rooting out the rest. Although it was a continual battle against weeds, the greens I had put in that spring were looking lush and healthy—and the dewberries had been corralled to the banks of Dewberry Creek, which ran along the back side of the property. The peach trees in the small orchard had been cloaked in gorgeous pink blossoms and now were laden with tiny fruits. In a few short months, I'd be trying out the honey-peach preserves recipe I'd found in my grandmother's handwritten cook-book, which was my most treasured possession. Sometimes, when I flipped through its yellowed pages, I almost felt as if my grandmother were standing next to me.

Now, I stifled a sigh of frustration as I watched the heifer browse the pasture. With time, I was hoping to get a cheese concern going; right now, I only had Blossom, but hopefully she'd calve a heifer, and with luck, I'd have two or three milkers soon. Money was on the tight side, and I might have to consider driving to farmers' markets in Austin to make ends meet—or maybe finding some kind of part-time job—but now that I'd found my way to Buttercup, I didn't want to leave.

I readjusted my ponytail—now that I didn't need to dress for work, I usually pulled my long brown hair back in the mornings—and mentally reviewed my to-do list. Picking dewberries was next, a delightful change from the more mundane tasks of my city days. I needed a few more batches of jam for Buttercup's Founders' Day Festival and Jam-Off, which was coming up in a few days. I'd pick before it got too hot; it had been a few days since I'd been down by the creek, and I hoped to harvest another several quarts.

Chuck, the small apricot rescue poodle who had been my constant companion for the past five years, joined me as I grabbed a pair of gardening gloves and the galvanized silver bucket I kept by the back door, then headed past the garden in the back and down to the creek, where the sweet smell of sycamores filled the air. I didn't let Chuck near Blossom—I was afraid she would do the same thing to him that she did to the milk bucket—but he accompanied me almost everywhere else on the farm, prancing through the tall grass, guarding me from wayward squirrels and crickets, and—unfortunately—picking up hundreds of burrs. I'd had to shave him within a week of arriving at the farm, and I was still getting used to having a bald poodle. This morning, he romped through the tall grass, occasionally stopping to sniff a particularly compelling tuft of grass. His pink skin showed through his clipped fur, and I found myself wondering if there was such a thing as doggie sunscreen.

The creek was running well this spring—we'd had plenty of rain, which was always welcome in Texas, and a giant bullfrog plopped into the water as I approached the mass of brambles with their dark, sweet berries. They were similar to the blackberries I bought in the store, but a bit longer, with a sweet-tart tang that I loved. I popped the first few in my mouth.

I went to work filling the bucket, using a stick to push the brambles aside, and had filled it about halfway when I heard the grumble of a motor coming up the long driveway. Chuck, who had been trying to figure out how to get to the fish that were darting in the deeper part of the creek, turned and growled. I shushed him as we headed back toward the farmhouse, the bucket swinging at my side.

A lanky man in jeans and a button-down shirt

was unfolding himself from the front seat of the truck as I opened the back gate. Chuck surged ahead of me, barking and growling, then slinking to my ankle when I shushed him with a sharp word.

"Can I help you?" I asked the man. He was in his mid-forties, with work-worn boots and the roughened skin of a man who'd spent most of his life outdoors.

"You Lucy Resnick?" he asked.

"I am," I said, putting down the bucket. Chuck growled again and put himself between us.

"Butch Simmons, Lone Star Exploration," the man said, squinting at me.

"Nice to meet you," I said, extending a hand. Chuck yipped, and I apologized.

"Good doggie," the man said, reaching down to let the poodle sniff him. Usually, that was all the little dog needed to become comfortable, but something about the man upset him. He growled, backing away.

"I don't know what's gotten into him," I said, scooping him up in my arms. "Can I help you with something?" I asked again, holding the squirming poodle tight.

"Mind if I take a few pictures? We're surveying the property before we start the exploration process."

"Exploration process?" I asked. "Didn't anyone tell you?"

"Tell me what?"

He turned his head and spit out a wad of snuff. I wrinkled my nose, revolted by the glob of brown goo on the caliche driveway. "We're drillin' for oil."

WANT TO READ MORE?

KILLER JAM

IS NOW AVAILABLE

OTHER BOOKS

KAREN MACINERNEY
BOOK LIST

Howling at the Moon
On the Prowl
Leader of the Pack

For more information and to buy go to
www.karenmacinerney.com.

ACKNOWLEDGMENTS

FIRST, MANY THANKS TO MY family, not just for putting up with me, but for continuing to come up with creative ways to kill people. (You should see the looks we get in restaurants.)

Special thanks to the MacInerney Mystery Mavens (who help with all manner of things, from covers to concepts), particularly Alicia Farage, Rudi Lee, Mandy Young Kutz, Kay Pucciarel-li, Priscilla Ormsby, Olivia Leigh Blacke, Samantha Mann, Pat Warren Tewalt, Norma Reed, Barb Wiesmann, and Chloe Shepard, for their careful reading of the manuscript. What would I do with-out you???

Kim Killion, as usual, did an amazing job on the cover design, and Randy Ladenheim-Gil's sharp editorial eye helped keep me from embarrassing myself. And finally, thank you to ALL of the wonderful readers who make Gray Whale Inn possible, especially my fabulous Facebook commu-nity at www.facebook.com/karenmacinerney. You keep me going!

ABOUT THE AUTHOR

KAREN IS THE HOUSEWORK-IMPAIRED, AWARD-WINNING author of multiple mystery series, and her victims number well into the double digits. She lives in Austin, Texas with her sassy family and a menagerie of animals, including twenty-three fish, two rabbits, and a rescue dog named Little Bit.

Feel free to visit Karen's web site at www. karenmacinerney.com, where you can download a free book and sign up for her Readers' Circle to receive subscriber-only short stories, deleted scenes, recipes and other bonus material. You can also find her on Facebook at www.facebook. com/AuthorKarenMacInerney or www.facebook. com/karenmacinerney (she spends an inordinate amount of time there). You are more than welcome to friend her there—and remind her to get back to work on the next book!

P. S. Don't forget to follow Karen on BookBub to get newsflashes on new releases!

Made in the USA
Middletown, DE
27 July 2018